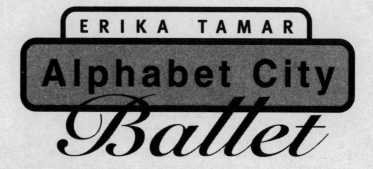

ERIKA TAMAR

Alphabet City Ballet

HarperTrophy®
A Division of HarperCollinsPublishers

Alphabet City Ballet
Copyright © 1996 by Erika Tamar

Library of Congress Cataloging-in-Publication Data
Tamar, Erika.
  Alphabet City ballet / Erika Tamar.
    p.   cm.
  Summary: Living in a poor Puerto Rican family complicates life for ten-year-old
Marisol when she realizes that pursuing her love for ballet may expose her brother
to danger.
  ISBN 0-06-027328-3. — ISBN 0-06-027329-1 (lib. bdg.)
  ISBN 0-06-440668-7 (pbk.)
  [1. Brothers and sisters—Fiction.   2. Ballet dancing—Fiction.   3. Puerto
Ricans—New York (N.Y.)—Fiction.   4. New York (N.Y.)—Fiction.]   I. Title.
PZ7.T159Al   1996   96-882
[Fic]—dc20   CIP
                                                                         AC

Typography by Darcy Soper
❖
First Harper Trophy edition, 1997

Visit us on the World Wide Web!
http://www.harperchildrens.com

For Patricia Lakin,
with heartfelt thanks

Sometimes Marisol let her feelings go bubbling out without thinking and then she wanted to disappear down a crack in the sidewalk. Like last Sunday outside East River Park. She had to stick with her big brother Luis on Sundays because Papi worked a double shift in the restaurant uptown. So Luis was hanging out with his friends and this guy Eddie had a boom box playing salsa. Some of the guys were shuffling to the beat, so, honest, it wasn't just *her*. But the music was popping inside her, sweeping her along, and she swayed with it. Her blood was sizzling with the beat; she whirled and whirled and clapped her hands double-time above her head and—

"Cut it out," Luis muttered under his breath.

Marisol stopped short and there were her arms, foolishly stuck up in the air for no good reason. And Luis looked away real fast, like he didn't want to know her, and got busy talking to the guys. Oh, snap, Marisol thought, I did it again!

Why did she always have to plunge right in, talk or dance or whatever, without thinking first! Eddie's box was still blasting, but she made up her mind she wouldn't ever move a muscle, no matter how much the music pulled at her. She was ten, too old to make a spectacle of herself.

She'd learn to be as cool and controlled as Luis. She watched him. He was slouched against the fence, slicking his hair back while he talked.

The boys were eyeing the low-slung shiny black car at the curb. It had to cost a fortune, Marisol thought. It belonged to that man called Tito and he was richer than God. She'd see him on Loisada, walking his German shepherd and wearing a long black leather coat. You could tell his leather was the soft-as-butter kind. And the way he went by, like he owned the street . . . No one would lay a hand on Tito's car, that was for sure.

They were talking and talking and talking. Marisol shifted her weight from foot to foot. It was cold for September. She could hear the wind rustling the scraggly bushes. How long was Luis going to hang out, anyway? Daylight was getting shorter every day; lights were already flickering on at the Avenue D projects. They were supposed to be home and safely locked in before dark, Papi said. And she had to pee.

She tugged at the sleeve of Luis's sweatshirt.

He swatted her hand off like he'd swat a fly and kept on talking. ". . . and anyway, a Lamborghini's better 'cause—"

She tugged again.

"What?" he snarled.

"When are we going home?" she said.

"In a minute." He turned back to the guys. "No competition, 'cause—"

"Give me the keys," Marisol said.

"Papi wants you staying with me. . . . Hey, listen, if I was racing—"

"Why can't you just give me the keys?" Marisol said.

"Wait a minute! I'm leaving in a minute!" He kept his face stony like always, but she knew he wished she wasn't around. ". . . if I was racing, that's the machine, man. I'd—"

When he was with his friends, Marisol thought, his minute was in Puerto Rican time and could last half an hour.

The autumn chill creeping under her sweater made the urge worse. She was embarrassed, but finally she had to whisper to him, "I gotta go."

"Okay, okay, all right." He sighed from the bottom of his sneakers. "Later, guys . . ."

They walked west past Avenue D. Marisol looked up at him. "Are you mad?"

"No," he said, "but you keep interrupting."

"I don't need to tag along next Sunday," Marisol said. "I'm doing something with my Big Sister."

"You like her?" Luis asked.

"Yeah, she's fun."

"She's a cop!"

"She's nice."

"She's still a cop," Luis said.

"So? Cops are okay."

"Yeah," Luis said, "tell me about it."

Something happened to Luis last summer. Some cops stopped him in the street for no good reason, and frisked him up against the wall, just like on TV. Everybody on the street that day was mad and yelling; Luis Perez was no troublemaker, they had him mixed up with someone else! Everybody knew he worked at the Isla Verde Superette every day after school, and Mr. Rivera even said he was a hard worker, and dependable.

Everyone liked him. On summer Sundays, when his team played baseball in East River Park, the cheers would go "Luis! Luis!" and Marisol would explode with feeling so proud. He was only fifteen, but he was a better athlete than lots of the older guys. He was good-looking, too—more than once, women in the neighborhood teased, "*Ay*, those eyelashes wasted on a boy!"

It wasn't just because he was her brother, he *was* special. Marisol glanced up at him. She hated having him think she was a burden, dragging him down on his day off.

"I don't know why Papi makes me stay with you," she said. "I can take care of myself."

"Yeah, I know," Luis said. "Papi's too careful."

That was the truth, Marisol thought. It was because he was trying to raise them right, all by himself. A lot of people had said he couldn't do it, not without a woman in the house and keeping his shifts uptown at the same time. But Mrs. Garcia had helped until Marisol was old enough for the after-school program and it had all worked out. Except for not having a mother, so that's why she got a Big Sister, 'cause Papi thought she ought to have someone to ask about woman things. She knew all those things—he thought she was still five!

"Following you around all day is so dumb." She kind of liked hanging out with Luis, but it would be better if it was his choice.

"Hey, I don't love it, either. But Papi said."

They were both stuck obeying his rules, Marisol thought.

"When I'm away and working uptown, I got to trust you're doing what I tell you even if I'm not there." Papi kept making that same speech. "It's hard on everybody without Mami, so you both got to hold up your end or else this family falls apart."

"Mami." Marisol couldn't call her that because she'd never really known her, she'd died so long ago. She'd say "my mother" or "Maria." In the wedding photo in the living room, she was beautiful, with a sweet smile. Luis looked something like her, Marisol thought; she didn't at all. But she wasn't sure—a photograph was only one second and sometimes people looked altogether different in real life. Luis remembered, enough to miss her, so Marisol couldn't ask him much—his face would get closed up.

In some ways, she was more like Papi, Marisol thought. They let their feelings out all over the place, even if they didn't mean to. Man, if Papi was mad, you knew it! But he was more interested in Luis's things. He played soccer with Luis any time he had a chance.

She'd overheard Papi talking on the front stoop. He'd sighed and said, "Raising a girl is harder." Why did he say that?

She was pretty sure Papi loved her, though. If there was a fire in the house, Papi would save her, even if maybe he'd save Luis first.

"Luis?"

"What?"

They were on Avenue C now, past the bodega, half a block from the apartment.

"If there was a fire in the house . . ."

"Enough with the fires," Luis said. He jiggled the keys impatiently. "Forget about it."

She wouldn't ever forget the night the fire-engine sirens woke her up, even though it was a long time ago. She'd seen it all from her window—smoke pouring from the building across the street, licks of orange flame, screams, people running out in their underwear. Later she found out a man had died. Some of the people had to go live in the homeless shelter.

"We're not gonna have a fire," Luis said.

"I'm just saying if. If there was a fire, would you save me?"

"Sure." He said it too easy, he wasn't even thinking.

"I mean, if it was *dangerous*, would you save me? If you were scared you'd get burned?"

"I don't get scared," Luis said. "Sure, I'd save you. I'd save everybody—you, the goldfish, everybody, okay?"

That was the test to see if someone *really* loved you, Marisol thought, if they'd risk their own life for you. Papi would. She didn't know about Luis.

It happened again: Marisol blurted something out without thinking, and this time she had the whole class laughing at her! From now on, she'd make sure to keep herself in control all the time.

It was all because of that stupid dream. Well, no, she couldn't call it stupid, because it was wonderful. And it felt so real, it was hard to tell where real life had ended and the dream had started. . . .

Marisol had stretched under her covers in the quiet time just before night turns into morning. Across the room, Luis was breathing softly, deep in his sleep. In the half-light, Marisol got up and tiptoed into the long narrow hall. She took a tiptoe step and—her foot stayed in the air! Another—and she was floating in the hall! She flew low, down to one end of the hall and then back to the other.

"Luis!" Marisol shouted. "Papi! Luis! Watch me!" But they were fast asleep.

Marisol flew back and forth, back and forth. It was so easy. She only had to kick her legs a bit. She could steer by shifting her shoulders. But Marisol kept bumping against the ceiling, so she flew out the front door and high over the stoop. She flew above Loisada Avenue and around the corner. The gray morning air was warm and soft and the moon was a fading sliver in the sky. She floated gently past third-floor fire escapes and window boxes trailing morning glories. The bodega was still dark.

Marisol spread her arms and soared with the wind. She rolled over a playful breeze and watched the sun come up in a great burst of color. Sunbeams rippled on the East River. A flock of seagulls followed a tugboat that was pulling a barge.

She flew over East Houston Street, where vendors were setting up tables with many-colored piles of clothing. The city was waking up and people hurried underground to the subway. Some men were playing baseball in the grass near the river. The outfielder looked way up for a fly ball, but when he saw Marisol he forgot to catch it. Home run! Olé! She couldn't wait to tell Papi and Luis.

Marisol somersaulted in the air, whooshed high into the sky and drifted on a soft white cloud. Floating . . .

In school that morning, the dream was still strong in Marisol's mind. She was supposed to be doing her arithmetic, but she didn't feel like it. She thought about how fine it felt to float free. She remembered the fuzzy damp of the cloud and she wished she could spread her arms and soar.

Mrs. Lonigan was a nice teacher. She didn't yell much, even when Marisol didn't do her homework and forgot her pencils. Between lessons, Mrs. Lonigan asked good questions to get the class talking about things. The term had just started, and Mrs. Lonigan said she wanted to get to know every single one of them. Marisol thought that was nice.

That morning, Marisol heard Mrs. Lonigan ask, "Does anyone know what they want to do—?"

And Marisol blurted out, forgetting to raise her hand first, "I want to fly!"

Everyone laughed at her.

"I want to be a secretary," Dolores said.

And then Marisol realized Mrs. Lonigan was asking what they wanted to do when they grew up.

"Marisol wants to be a pigeon!" Joseph yelled. And everyone laughed again. Even those dumb kids from the shelter who smelled bad—they had no business laughing at her!

Mrs. Lonigan was nice. She said, "Maybe Marisol would like to be a pilot—"

But the boys kept calling her "bird-girl" all morning.

Even Marisol's best friend, Gloria, thought it was weird. "What did you say that for?"

"I don't know," Marisol mumbled. And she swore to herself that she'd never do anything stupid again.

After lunch, Mrs. Lonigan told them they had a very special opportunity today to try out for ballet. There was this ballet company's school that was giving out two scholarships in their neighborhood, that meant it was free, so if anyone wanted to try out, they could go to the gym in the afternoon.

Marisol sighed. She wasn't about to start *dancing* in front of anyone again! She could just see Luis rolling his eyes at her. And she sure didn't know how to dance ballet. But she'd seen a ballet dancer on TV and it had looked wonderful. . . .

When it was their class's turn, Gloria said, "Oh, come on, Marisol, let's go." All the girls were going down to the gym. Mrs. Lonigan said the boys should go, too, because it was a special opportunity, but none of them would. Marisol didn't want to stay behind in the classroom with the boys, so she followed the line downstairs. But she'd remember to keep herself tightly in check; this could be a special opportunity to make a fool of herself again!

The girls had to take their shoes and socks off and line up at one end of the gym. A man and a lady sat at a table, watching and making notes. There was another lady walking around and telling them what to do next.

She had jet-black hair piled in a bun on top of her head and very pale skin and dark-red lipstick. She was thin and the skirt of her black dress fluttered around her when she walked; Marisol thought that looked beautiful. When she told them to walk across to the table one at a time, Marisol would have wanted to walk just like her, but jeans couldn't flutter. It felt funny to walk across and have them watching. A card with the number 12 on it hung from her neck and bounced against her chest. When she reached the table, they told her to raise her leg and arch her foot. The man looked at it and started scribbing something. None of this stuff seemed to be about dancing.

Back in line, Gloria whispered, "Were you nervous?"

Marisol shrugged. She didn't know exactly how she felt, but she wanted whatever that lady was giving out.

Jennifer wouldn't walk across at all. Francie and Dolores had giggling fits.

Then the lady said, "Thank you. One moment, please."

She went to the table and looked at the man's notes. Then she looked at her own, frowning. She talked to the other two for a moment and crossed something out.

Marisol watched her move back to the center. Her legs were long and slim, but all muscle, like a runner's; how did she manage to float when she walked? And the way she held herself—so proud, even arrogant. She wasn't like anybody else.

"Of course, ballet requires a certain body type, high arches and . . ." The lady gestured in the air and even that was graceful. ". . . and it's not suitable for everyone. I'd like the numbers I call to stay, and the others please return to your classroom. But thank you all."

"Call me," Gloria whispered, "call me."

The lady read from the sheet of paper in her hand.

"Number three," she said, loud and clear.

It was that Haitian shelter kid, Desirée, the one who never said a word. Marisol heard her soft gasp.

"Number six."

"Number seven."

So far, she was picking all skinny girls. Good, Marisol was skinny!

"Number eleven."

She was calling out the numbers in order! Now twelve, Marisol thought, please twelve! She clasped Gloria's hand and held it tight.

"Number twelve."

"I got it!" Marisol whooped.

"No you didn't," Gloria said. "They're only picking two, remember? And from Mrs. Cornell's class, too." She sounded mean, and Marisol realized Gloria's number had been passed by.

"Oh," Marisol said. "I'm sorry—"

"Who cares about stupid ballet? I sure don't! I think she's rude."

Marisol couldn't keep down her joy at being picked. It felt like winning!

"And number fifteen. I'm sorry we can't take everyone. Thank you, girls."

The others filed out in a raggedy, muttering group.

Only six were left. Marisol, Desirée, Olga, Anita, Carmen, and Stacy. They moved closer to each other. Now what? Marisol thought.

Suddenly music flooded the gym. It wasn't anything

Marisol knew. It was a slow and swooping melody.

"I want to see you move with the music," the lady
said. "Do whatever you wish." She half smiled. "As long
as you don't bump into each other."

They all looked at each other. And Marisol was
thinking she wasn't about to make a jerk of herself again.
She'd watch and see what the others did.

"Come on now," the lady said impatiently. "Let's go."

No one moved. Finally Olga was the brave one; she
hesitantly began to twirl. The others followed, all six of
them turning like tops in one corner. All that twirling was
making Marisol dizzy and it was getting boring, too; the
music wanted more, but Marisol didn't want to mess up
and do anything weird.

"Don't you feel the music?" the lady said. "Perhaps
some big moves or jumps or—"

So they all started jumping around the room and six
pairs of feet thudded on the gym floor.

But then the music was soaring and it carried Marisol
and made her leap higher and higher and she was flying. It
was wonderful! She stretched her arms wide and swooped
up, up to tiptoe, yearning to be free of the ground, whirling,
leaping, lost in a dream.

The tape ended abruptly. Bewildered, Marisol stopped.
She caught her breath. If this was ballet, this was all she
wanted!

The lady glanced her way for a second, but Marisol
couldn't tell anything at all from her face.

Marisol saved her news until Papi came home that night and then she just about exploded with it.

"Slow down," Papi said. "What scholarship?"

"To *ballet* school! I just told you." She followed Papi as he took off his jacket and hung it in the closet. "The lady picked out six girls to stay, and guess what, I was one of them!"

Papi stretched. "Hold it, I got to wash up."

Marisol stood in front of the closed bathroom door. She waited impatiently for the sound of running water to stop.

Luis pulled at her arm. "Give him a little privacy, why don't you?"

Marisol sighed and took three deliberate steps backward.

"What did she say when she picked you?" Luis asked.

"She let me try out some more. Like in a small group."

"So you don't even know if you have it."

"But I might."

"What's the big deal, anyway?" Luis asked. "Since when do you care about ballet?"

"Since now." The truth was, she'd never thought of dance lessons. When one of the Miss America girls on TV danced in a tutu for her talent, it was beautiful; she'd wanted her to win. When Papi took them to Radio City last Christmas, she'd wished she was one of the Rockettes. And when the music was hot, she couldn't keep from dancing, and that's how she embarrassed Luis in front of his friends. But she'd never even thought of getting real lessons before. All of a sudden, it was possible!

"You have to dance on the tip of your toes," Luis said.

"So? They'll show me how."

Finally, Papi came out of the bathroom.

"Bad day today," Papi said. "A party of eight, they sat at the table for hours, wanting this and that—and then they stiffed me. Foreigners. They think everything's *service compris*."

"When the tip is part of the bill, right, Papi?" Luis said.

"Right. That's the way they do in Europe. The minute I see foreigners come in, I want to tell them—"

"Why don't you?" Luis asked.

"Because the new manager's an ass and he thinks I'm there for my—"

"Papi," Marisol broke in, "about the scholarship—"

"Who'd be giving away free lessons and why?" Papi said. "There's got to be a catch." He was in a rotten mood.

"Could be they up the price by like fifty dollars," Luis said, "and then they tell you it's a fifty-dollar scholarship and you got to come up with the rest. Like bait and switch."

"It's not like that," Marisol said. "It's free! Mrs. Lonigan said—"

But Papi was rummaging through the refrigerator, and they weren't listening to her at all.

She had expected Papi to be excited about it. Because he was a *wonderful* dancer himself. On summer Sundays everyone hung out at the picnic area in East River Park, the one next to the ball field near the Tenth Street overpass. There was the smell of roasting pork on the river breeze and you could buy *alcapurrias* to eat and Maria Lopez sold rum and cola to the grown-ups when she wasn't dancing to the merengue or *bomba y plena* blasting from D.J. Julio's stereo. The time Papi had Sunday off, he went there with them and danced his head off. Marisol was so proud of the way he moved. He was the best dancer, and all the women crowded around to dance with him. Especially that Nina Matos with the bleached-blond hair who thought she was so hot. Anyway, Marisol thought Papi would at least be interested in her dancing.

She wouldn't say another word. She'd wait until she got the scholarship and then she'd tell them and *then* they'd get excited.

• • •

Marisol rushed to school on Tuesday morning. She couldn't wait to hear.

All the girls in Mrs. Cornell's class had tried out, and Mrs. Delano's class, too. Olga said *eight* girls from Mrs. Delano's class had their numbers called. Marisol hoped, she hoped. . . .

But Mrs. Lonigan didn't say anything; she just went right on with arithmetic. By the time they got to the multiplication drills, Marisol couldn't stand not knowing for one more second!

"Who did the ballet lady pick?"

"How many times have I told you, Marisol, you can't call out like that." Mrs. Lonigan was frowning. "You *must* raise your hand! Now open to page fifty-three."

That's the way it went on Tuesday, and Wednesday, too. Not a word about the ballet. Marisol couldn't stop thinking about it. She had black hair like the ballet lady's, but hers was way too short; she'd never get it into a topknot like that. Marisol tugged hard at strands of her hair and wished it would grow.

"Marisol," Mrs. Lonigan said, "the next sentence, please."

Oh, snap, she had lost her place in the reader, and she was in trouble again.

On Thursday Mrs. Lonigan talked about double negatives, and they had to write in their notebooks: "I don't have *any* apples" instead of "I don't have no apples." What's the difference? Marisol thought. Luis and Papi said it the wrong way, but everyone understood what they meant; that's the way real people talked. She didn't like apples much. Sometimes Papi bought a juicy ripe mango at the Isla Verde.

Grammar was boring. Marisol squirmed in her chair and leaned over toward Gloria.

"When are they gonna tell us?" Marisol whispered. "About ballet school?"

"I bet they don't take nobody," Gloria said.

"It was supposed to be *two!*" Marisol whispered urgently. "Mrs. Lonigan said! . . . Didn't she?"

Gloria shrugged and continued writing in her notebook.

She did say two, Marisol thought. She chewed on her pencil. Two from the neighborhood.

That's when Mrs. Lonigan said, "Marisol, see me after school, please."

Marisol's heart leaped. She had been picked, that's what it was! Mrs. Lonigan didn't want to tell her in front of everybody because she was the only one from the class! She couldn't wait for school to be over. She was floating in a dream and counting the minutes. Finally the bell rang. The class rushed out and Marisol flew to Mrs. Lonigan's desk.

"Did I—" Marisol started breathlessly and then she came to earth with a terrible thump. Mrs. Lonigan didn't have a good-news smile.

"Marisol, you didn't have your homework today . . ."

Marisol almost felt like crying, but she was too grown-up for that.

". . . and it's the second time this week."

"Oh" was all she could say. She was going to do her homework after dinner last night, but then Papi came home and he brought leftover pastries from the restaurant, they were so good, they were called napoleons in honor of a very short Frenchman, Papi said. Later, Papi felt like taking out his guitar and he taught them one of the old songs from when he used to be a musician. It was about green eyes, it went ". . . el tema dulce de mi canción . . ." Papi was so much fun when he was singing like that—and she forgot about the homework. Anyway, Luis hardly ever did his; he said it had nothing to do with anything.

"You're a very bright girl," Mrs. Lonigan was saying, "and that's why I'm so disappointed. You're not paying attention, you were talking to Gloria and not letting her work, you call out in class whenever you feel like it and—"

"Sorry," Marisol mumbled.

"I know you could do better. I'd like to see your mother and—"

"There's only my father."

"All right, your father, then." Mrs. Lonigan was writing a note. "Here, ask him to call me and we'll set up—"

"He can't come," Marisol said. "He can't take off work." Papi would be mad! He'd lose a lot of money. And he'd be disappointed in her too.

"At his convenience, Marisol, but . . . I'll arrange something, but I want to . . . You have no self-discipline and—"

"Please, Mrs. Lonigan, give me another chance."

"It's not a punishment, it's to help you to—"

"You're not making *Joey's* mother come to school." Joey was really bad; he ran around the classroom and threw things.

Mrs. Lonigan shook her head. "You have potential, Marisol, and if there's a problem—"

Marisol didn't know what *potential* meant, but she didn't feel like asking just then.

"I'll be good, Mrs. Lonigan. I promise."

Mrs. Lonigan didn't say anything.

"There's no problem, honest. I'll do better."

"Marisol—"

"Can my big brother come instead?" Marisol asked. Luis wouldn't care.

"How old is he?"

"Fifteen."

"No. I want to see your father."

"He *can't* miss a shift. *Please*, Mrs. Lonigan."

"I think it's— Does he know you get homework every night?"

"I'll do it, I promise. From now on."

"What does your father do, Marisol?"

"He works in a big restaurant uptown, up on Fifty-eighth Street. You should see it, it's two-star. Tips are lots better at night, but he only works days because of me and Luis, so he can't just skip a day and—"

"All right." Mrs. Lonigan sighed. For a moment, she looked like she was sorry for them and Marisol felt funny. She wished she could take back that stuff about tips; why did she always have to talk first and think later! Nobody had to feel sorry, 'cause they weren't poor; they got everything they needed, and napoleons, too. They weren't poor like those shelter people.

"All right." Mrs Lonigan slowly crumpled the note. "I'll expect a big improvement."

"Thanks. I mean it, thanks!" Marisol started to go; she thought she'd better leave fast before Mrs. Lonigan changed her mind—but she couldn't keep herself from turning back. "Mrs. Lonigan?"

"Yes?"

"About the ballet scholarship." Marisol focused on the teacher's shiny gold earrings. "Did anyone—?"

"Yes? What is it?"

Marisol shrugged, her hands clutched together. "Did they . . . uh . . . like, did they . . . pick anybody yet?"

"No, not yet. I haven't heard anything."

Relief flooded Marisol like sunshine and she broke into a huge smile. "I still have a chance!" she blurted.

"You do, and so do the other girls. You know they can't take everyone."

"When are they gonna tell you? What's taking them so long?"

Mrs. Lonigan half smiled. "It's only been three days."

"It feels like forever ago. I can't wait!"

Mrs. Lonigan studied her. "Well, forget about it for now and concentrate on your schoolwork. That's much more important for you."

Teacher or not, Marisol knew with all her heart that Mrs. Lonigan was wrong about that.

When the after-school program was over, Marisol went to the Isla Verde to wait for Luis to finish work. He got off at five, so she never had to wait long; usually, they went home together.

Though she mostly liked the after-school program—they did art and if the weather was nice they played dodgeball—sometimes she just felt like being home in the afternoon. But every time she said something to Papi, he said no. And if she asked why, he said, "Because that's the way I want it."

She passed the steel shutter that was pulled down over the big side window of the Isla Verde and looked at the mural painted on it. Chico's murals were on walls all over the neighborhood. You didn't even need to see the Chico on the bottom; you could always tell they were his because he was *really* good. The one at the Isla Verde showed a bright green island in a sea of blue. Papi said it was the shape of Puerto Rico. There were red flowers, called flamboyán, all around the edges. Marisol knew Chico to say hello to, but they never talked because he was lots older.

Marisol went into the superette and looked down the aisles for Luis. Usually he was stacking the shelves or sweeping up, but she didn't see him. She went over to the gray-haired cashier.

"Hi, Mr. Bonilla."

"¡Ah, muñequita! ¿Qué pasa?"

"Nothing much. Where's my brother?"

"He had an errand. He said to wait, back in a second."

"Oh. Okay."

Marisol shifted restlessly from foot to foot. More than a second was going by, that was for sure.

"Which way did he go?" she asked.

"Up Loisada."

She left the Isla Verde and started up the block. She saw Luis's red jacket across the avenue and started to run over. She stopped short. Luis was with that man Tito! She saw Luis handing over a brown paper bag. Then Tito was giving him something. They were talking. What was Luis doing talking to Tito? She was scared. She stayed put where she was.

Finally Luis crossed over. He looked surprised to see her.

"What are you doing here?" he said.

"I saw you with Tito. I saw you."

"What're you doing, spying on me?"

"I was waiting for you."

"He gave me twenty bucks! Twenty bucks, just like that!"

"Oh Luis, don't, please." Marisol felt like crying. Chico's other murals came into her mind: "José, R.I.P." with a painting of José just the way he used to look, but with a crown of thorns on his head. R.I.P. meant Rest in Peace. And then there was "Bobby. We love you. R.I.P." Bobby was only seventeen and he got shot. It was all about drugs, and everyone knew why Tito was so rich.

"Luis! Just say no," Marisol said. That was on another of Chico's paintings, that and "Drugs Kill." She felt her heart thumping. Not Luis, not her brother!

"Hey, Marisol, wait a minute. He asked me to get him a six-pack of Coke. I mean Coca-Cola. He gave me a tip, that's all."

"Why did he ask you?"

"'Cause he was thirsty, I don't know. I swear to God, Marisol, that's all it was. Come on, let's go."

They headed toward home.

"He knew me," Luis said. "He knew my name and everything. He likes me."

"Papi says he's evil."

"You should've seen the roll of bills he pulled out of his pocket. I bet there were hundreds! He peeled off the twenty like it was nothing."

"The way Johnny Castro is, Papi says that's Tito's fault." Johnny lived upstairs from them; he was a good-natured teenager with the warmest smile, but now he was all messed up.

"I'd never be dumb enough to use the stuff. If I worked for Tito—"

"Don't work for Tito! Luis, don't!"

"I'm not about to. I was just saying if. He didn't ask me to or nothing; we were talking baseball. I brought him the six-pack, that's all it was."

"Do you promise that's all?" She couldn't keep her lips from quivering.

He put his arm around her shoulder. "Easy, Marisol, it's all right. I promise. Anyway, if I was working for Tito, you think I'd be sweeping the Isla Verde?"

"No," she said in a small voice.

"Okay, that proves it." They had reached the house. Marisol followed Luis up the stairs. At the second-floor landing, he turned back to her.

"Don't say anything to Papi."

Marisol hesitated.

"All I did was talk to the guy, but you know Papi. Don't tell him, okay?"

"Okay."

She hoped Tito wouldn't ask Luis to bring him any more sodas. She hoped he wouldn't ever talk to Luis again.

Marisol had a little skip in her walk as she and Jeanne Carlsen crossed Avenue C. They always did fun things.

Marisol had been disappointed when she'd first met Jeanne. She'd hoped her Big Sister would be pretty. And that first Sunday, three weeks ago, it was awkward because they were both figuring out what to talk about. But now Marisol liked Jeanne's face, even though her nose was too wide and freckly. Jeanne's smile showed too many teeth, but it was warm and her eyes smiled too. Jeanne kept her hair pulled back with a rubber band in a plain ponytail; the color was pretty, Marisol thought loyally, kind of ashy blond.

"Have you ever been to Orleon?" Jeanne asked.

"No."

"I think you'll like it. Their brunch is a little different, you know? Pumpkin pancakes with some kind of cinnamon sauce, or—"

"I'll have that," Marisol said. "I *love* cinnamon!"

"Me too," Jeanne said. "Whenever I was sick, when I was a little girl, my mom made cinnamon toast for me."

"Oh, yum," Marisol said.

"The only thing, Orleon gets crowded and the waiters are slow as molasses, but we've got time."

Orleon was a restaurant between First and Second avenues, where all those restaurants were. It was funny, it was only three blocks west, but it was like a different town, full of yuppies and hippies or whatever they were. Gentrified, Pop said. That meant buildings over there got fixed up so the landlords could charge more rent. And then a little way over was Ukrainian—Surma, the Blue and Gold Tavern, the Ukrainian museum, the Ukrainian church, and the old ladies with broad cheekbones and flowered kerchiefs. Well, even her own neighborhood turned into a whole different world at night, when the daytime people stayed home and locked up, and the nighttime people came out; that's when you might get caught in cross fire.

That's all outsiders thought of when they heard "Alphabet City": drugs and shootings. That's why some people said they lived in the "far East Village" or "Lower East Side." But Marisol liked "Alphabet City," a name just for her neighborhood with its letter avenues. And she liked that her street had two street signs: "Avenue C" and "Loisada Avenue." "Loisada" was supposed to be for the way Puerto Ricans said "Lower East Side," and that made it especially her own.

They had reached Avenue B and Jeanne was heading toward A. Marisol tugged at her hand. "Wait, you want to see a garden before we go?" She wanted Jeanne to see how nice her neighborhood was. "Right over on Sixth Street. It's beautiful."

"The movie starts at one, so we'd better go straight to Orleon," Jeanne said.

"Okay, next time I'll show you all the gardens. Jardin des Amies still has the roses blooming, you should see it. And the Garden of Happiness has benches under an arbor, so it's nice and shady in the summertime and then there's the People's Garden, it's big and it has a youth group and—"

Jeanne laughed. "Sounds like a whole Sunday's worth. Maybe next time—not next Sunday, because I've got the rotation, but the one after that."

"All right, but not too long, 'cause they're not as flowery when it gets cold."

Papi said Puerto Rico was a beautiful island, so the people created little pieces of it in empty lots right here in Alphabet City. Papi said you'd think you were back in Santurce when you were sitting in the little garden on their block.

"Unless you'd rather skip the movie today?" Jeanne asked.

"No, let's see it." Marisol didn't want to hurt Jeanne's feelings. It was some Disney thing and they were always too cute, but it seemed like Jeanne was into it. Marisol liked real-life movies, about gunfights and car chases, or about real animals.

At Orleon, Marisol picked a mushroom omelette instead of the pumpkin pancakes because the waiter said it was great and he was right. She took a taste of Jeanne's pancakes and they were good too. She liked this place. There was a good coffee smell in the air. It was nice of Jeanne to treat her and even spend her Sunday off doing something with her. On a nice day like this, most grown-ups would find a million other things to do instead of hanging out with a kid.

"Why did you want to be a Big Sister?" Marisol asked.

"Well, because . . . mostly, because I like children and . . . I thought it would be fun to have a little sister. And guess what? It is."

"For me too!" There were french fries on the side and Marisol nibbled on one. "Do you want to have kids of your own?"

"Sure, someday."

"Do you have a boyfriend?"

"No, not right now."

What was the matter with guys, anyway? Marisol thought. Being pretty wasn't everything. "You oughtta have lots of boyfriends. You're *nice*."

"Some men get scared off by a policewoman."

"Well, you wouldn't carry a gun on a date, would you? So that's dumb."

Jeanne smiled as she cut her pancakes.

Jeanne was a cop; that's what Marisol had been thinking about all morning. A cop would know what to do—she could ask her. And then she thought, better not say anything. But . . .

Marisol moved the last bits of egg around with her fork. "Jeanne, if somebody does favors for a dope dealer, could he get in trouble? I mean, if people see them together."

Jeanne stopped eating and looked at her. "What kind of favors?"

"Like getting things for him, soda and stuff, but like somebody might start hanging out with him and getting friendly."

"That's not a good idea. Marisol, is this somebody you know?"

She trusted Jeanne herself, Marisol thought, but she couldn't trust her for Luis. "No, I saw it on TV. Never mind."

Jeanne was still looking at her. She had to change the subject, fast.

"Uh . . . how did you decide to become a cop?"

"I hated working in an office—that's what I did for a while, secretarial work—I hated it. I wanted to do something to help people and . . ." Jeanne shrugged. "I'm athletic and I knew I could pass the physical."

"It's exciting, right?"

"It's not glamorous like on TV. A lot of paperwork and a lot of waiting around. But there are times. When you stop a bad guy, you feel very good."

"Did you ever kill anybody?"

"No, thank God. There are times you have to draw your gun and the truth is, you're scared stiff. Scared you might have to shoot and scared someone's going to shoot you first."

"If there's a big drug king walking around in his leather coat, and everybody knows it, how come the cops don't arrest him? Are they scared of him?"

"Everybody knowing is one thing, but proving it is something else." Jeanne studied Marisol. "The big dealers are careful; they get underage kids selling for them."

"Oh."

"Marisol, is there something you want to tell me?"

"No. I was thinking about a TV show, that's all." She couldn't tell Jeanne. She couldn't tell Papi; not telling him had almost hurt her throat! Luis said he wasn't doing anything. But she wished someone would take Tito off the street.

"Marisol?"

She had to talk about something else, quick. "I tried out for a ballet scholarship last week. For the Manhattan Ballet School."

"Manhattan Ballet School! Do you know that's the school for a *very* famous ballet company?"

She'd never even thought about it being something famous! "I might not get it. I don't know." It was scary to want something so much. Almost more than anything. Almost more than wishing for Luis to be safe.

"Ballet takes a lot of discipline," Jeanne said.

"Discipline?"

"I mean self-discipline. My friend Karen in high school took ballet; she had classes every day while the rest of us were hanging out. She had to do these exercises, over and over and over, and she was always aching somewhere. Finally she quit."

Marisol sighed. Mrs. Lonigan had told her she had no self-discipline. Mrs. Lonigan had used those exact words. She probably didn't have a chance.

Sometimes life sneaked a surprise up on you just when you weren't expecting it, Marisol thought. Like last summer at East River Park, Mr. Galarza's number came up when he was turned away with his eyes on Ninette Bonilla in her pink halter top. Everybody at the numbers game was yelling to let him know; he got fifty dollars the one time he wasn't paying attention!

Well, that Monday morning, Marisol was busy talking to Gloria. Gloria said her uncle was coming up from Puerto Rico to live with them and he was only thirteen years old, younger than Luis! Marisol was asking how come she had such a young uncle; it was interesting and she hardly heard Mrs. Lonigan's voice in the background—until Mrs. Lonigan rapped a ruler on her desk.

"Marisol! I said sit down."

"Oh," Marisol mumbled. "Sorry." She scrambled to her seat. Oh, snap, she was in trouble again!

"Do I have *everyone's* attention now?"

All the kids looked up at Mrs. Lonigan. Except for

Joey, who was rolling some kind of metal ball back and forth on his desk. Forever after, Marisol would remember the rumble of metal against wood at that moment.

"I have a very special announcement. The Manhattan Ballet School chose *both* scholarships from our class! Isn't that wonderful?"

The metal ball rolled. Somebody coughed. Marisol felt numb. She stared at Mrs. Lonigan's red-lipsticked mouth. There was the smell of tuna from somebody's lunch bag. There was the sound of rustling papers.

"Desirée and—"

A soft "oh" escaped from Desirée. Everyone turned to look at her and she tucked her chin down. Her eyes were big and round. They picked a *shelter* kid, Marisol thought.

"And . . ." Mrs. Lonigan continued. Time stopped. The teacher's lips were moving in slow motion.

". . . Marisol."

For a moment, she couldn't move at all. Then she threw her fists in the air and yelled "Me! I got it!" She felt her smile brimming over into tears.

This time, Mrs. Lonigan wasn't mad that she had called out.

"Congratulations, girls!" Mrs. Lonigan started to clap and encouraged the class to join in. "See me after school and I'll give you all the information. This is *very* exciting. All right now, let's get those readers open to page twenty-five and—Joey, stop that!—page twenty-five and . . ."

The rest of the school day went by in a sunshiney

blur. A little voice inside Marisol was singing, "So happy, so happy, so happy . . ."

"Mira." Marisol shoved the form in front of Papi on the kitchen table. "You have to sign, that's all. And I get to go every single Wednesday all year!" She had to raise her voice over the clatter of pots as Luis washed the dishes.

"They only took two from your whole school?" Papi smiled. "You must be some terrific dancer."

Marisol smiled back. "Just like my papi."

"Well, I never did no ballet."

Luis turned from the sink. "Yeah, picture Papi bouncing around in tights!"

Papi jumped up from the chair and began turning and clapping his hands and doing all this stuff! By the time he sat down again, they were all laughing.

"You shoulda seen, I was flying!" Marisol said. "I'll learn everything and I'll practice all the time and I'll—"

"Wait," Papi said. "It says here you gotta buy things."

"Just a leotard and tights and ballet slippers." Marisol looked at him anxiously. "That's not so much."

There was a little pause that made Marisol catch her breath before he said, "No, I guess not."

"They'll last all year, 'cause leotards stretch and my feet won't grow, I promise."

Papi smiled. "It's okay, I can spring for your ballet shoes. I'm proud of mi bailarina."

"The lessons are free. And it's famous. My Big Sister said."

"Mmm-hmm. I heard of it someplace."

"No kidding, it's famous?" Luis put in. "That's pretty good."

"'Cause it's the school for a ballet company and they perform at—"

Papi shushed her. "Wait, let me read the rest of this."

She was going to be a dancer. For real. She took a deep breath. Her stomach felt fluttery.

"Come on, you're supposed to dry," Luis said.

"In a minute, Papi and me are talking."

"You think you're a famous dancer, you can't get your hands wet?"

"In a minute!"

"Marisol—" Papi's voice had a bad-news sound.

"What? What's the matter?"

"Marisol, it says here . . . It says Wednesdays, four to five, at Lincoln Center."

Marisol shrugged, mystified. All of a sudden, he looked so sorrowful.

"I don't know how you're gonna get uptown," Papi said.

"The—the subway."

"You know you can't go by yourself."

"Then—I thought you— Can't you—"

"That's half a day. More than half a day. By the time I come get you, and take you home again after . . ." He reached for her hand on the kitchen table. "I wish I could, mi *vida*. I can't take off work."

"I'll go by myself. Nothing's gonna happen." The truth was, she didn't know how to get there, but she'd find out.

"No way."

"But it's important!"

"No way. You need to change to the Seven at Forty-second Street for the Broadway line and then . . . No. No little girl belongs traveling the subways alone."

"I'm no little girl," she wailed. "I'm old enough." She looked at Luis. She wished he'd tell that to Papi. But he was standing at the sink, silent, looking from one to the other.

Papi shook his head. "You're not walking from East Houston after dark."

"*Please*, Papi." She couldn't lose ballet school, not now, not after she'd hoped so hard and been so glad!

"I'm sorry." He sighed. "I wish I could. . . . There'll be other things."

"No, there won't!"

"Listen to me." He looked pained. "You have to know this: I'm doing the best I can."

Marisol bit her lip. Papi was looking so hurt, but he was still taking everything away from her.

"Please," she whispered. It was all she could say. "Please," like a prayer.

Papi looked away. He ran his hands through his hair.

The refrigerator hummed. The smell of cilantro from

their rice and beans dinner was still hanging in the air. The faucet squeaked as Luis turned it off.

"It would only be half a day," she pleaded.

His face tightened. "Did you hear me say no? My job's the most important thing around here."

Everything was important around here except her! "Just one afternoon—"

"Leave Papi alone." Luis's voice was harsh.

"What about Luis? Luis can take me!"

"Yeah, but—" Papi started.

"Wait a minute," Luis said. "I work afternoons, remember?"

"Tell him he has to," Marisol said.

"No, that's up to him."

"I don't have time. They want me at Isla Verde every day," Luis said. "There's plenty of guys would take my job in a second."

"But I won the scholarship," Marisol said. "I need you to take me."

"Well, I need a new mitt. I need a ten-speed bike. I need about a million things," Luis said. "So I'm not losing my job over some tippy-toe stuff." He tossed the dish towel to her.

She went to the sink. She dried the same plate over and over, automatically moving the towel in the same circle, her mind racing in all directions, looking for a way.

"What about Aunt Mercedes?"

"You want my sister to come all the way down from

the Bronx?" Papi asked incredulously. "What is she supposed to do with her own kids?"

Papi always told them to call Aunt Mercedes in case of emergency. Well, this was an emergency. It wasn't fair!

Luis cleared his throat. "She could walk home from East Houston. It's not like six o'clock is midnight."

"Past the *gente mala* that come out soon as the sun goes down? What's the matter with you?" Papi was good and mad now.

"It's no big deal," Luis said. "Some of them are cool guys."

Marisol looked at Luis fast. He was thinking about Tito, she knew it.

"She could take care of herself," Luis continued.

"I could take the subway," Marisol said, "and Luis could meet me at the station. Okay, Papi?"

"I don't know," Luis mumbled. "I might not have time."

"Papi, what if you took off work early and met me?" Marisol said. "Just a little early? Say yes."

Papi slapped the table. "Enough of this!" The chair banged as he jumped up. "I want some peace after a hard day!"

Marisol tugged at his sleeve as he passed her. "Sign the permission, okay? I got to bring it to school."

His jaw was set hard. "I said that's enough!"

He stalked into the living room. They heard him take out his guitar. He started playing. It wasn't one of his beautiful sweet songs. The chords were harsh.

"You made him feel bad," Luis said. "He can't do more than he can do. It wasn't worth it."

"I know! I'll ask Mrs. Garcia to take me to ballet!" Mrs. Garcia had taken care of her all that time when she was little. Her hair had turned almost all white now, but she could still—

"Don't ask her, she won't."

"She'd do that for me, she *loves* me. She always watched me and—"

"'Cause Papi paid her to."

"Papi paid her?" Mrs. Garcia, with her welcoming lap, Mrs. Garcia who made *arroz con dulce* especially for her. Marisol felt like the ground was crumbling under her feet. She turned her face away so Luis wouldn't see.

"Didn't you know? I'm not saying she don't like you, but . . . She watches Ninette Bonilla's kids now. Forget about it. Quit pestering everybody."

Marisol looked down at the floor. She ran her foot along a crack in the linoleum. "Papi'll listen to you. Tell him—"

"You got to know when to leave somebody alone."

"But it's my *dream*."

"Papi had dreams too. You don't remember back when he played at the café. He even auditioned for Puente one time."

"He did?"

"Dreams are smoke in the air. Nobody dreams about waiting tables, but that's what happens."

"I might be *great* at ballet. I don't know, but what if I am? They picked me, didn't they? I've *got* to go."

Luis shrugged.

If it was the other way around, Marisol thought, she would have helped him somehow. He didn't care about her at all.

Mrs. Lonigan stopped Marisol as the class was filing out at lunchtime.

"Do you have your permission slip?"

"Oh." Marisol hesitated. "I—I forgot it."

"I have to send it in for you, Marisol, so will you be sure to bring it tomorrow?"

Marisol shifted her eyes away from Mrs. Lonigan's. "Okay."

"Desirée, wait," Mrs. Lonigan called.

Desirée, startled, stopped on her way out.

"How about yours?" she asked. "Your permission slip for ballet class. Do you have it for me?"

Desirée shook her head.

"I can't understand you girls," Mrs. Lonigan said. "I really can't! Don't you appreciate how lucky you are to get this opportunity? The least you could do is follow through."

Marisol and Desirée stared at her mutely.

"You know, Marisol, I went out of my way for you. I said you were a good student; I said you'd keep up with your schoolwork, though I'm afraid that's stretching the truth. I did everything I could not to disqualify you."

Marisol felt her face getting hot. Mrs. Lonigan didn't need to lie for her! She could keep up with the school-work, easy, if she wanted to.

Mrs. Lonigan seemed to be waiting, so Marisol mumbled, "Thank you."

"But if you girls don't care enough to—"

"I do care!" Marisol said.

Mrs. Lonigan couldn't know how hard she was trying to find a way. Last night, she'd even phoned Jeanne Carlsen, though she knew it wasn't right to ask that much of a Big Sister. Jeanne had been nice about it, she wished she could help, but she had all those shifts.

"Then remember," Mrs. Lonigan was saying, "signed permission tomorrow."

"My mother," Desirée whispered, "she has to see."

"I gave you all the information; if there are any questions, tell her to call me."

Desirée nodded.

Mrs. Lonigan blew out an exasperated breath. "All right, girls, go down to lunch."

The rest of the class was already gone. Marisol went down the stairs to the lunchroom with Desirée following behind her. They didn't talk. Mostly the shelter kids stayed together.

Marisol wondered how it turned out to be the two of them; as far as she could see, there was nothing about them that was the least bit alike. Desirée was black and Haitian—she had an accent that made some of her r's sound like w's—and she was so shy, she hardly said two words. Marisol was Puerto Rican and white and she was never afraid to speak up; Mrs. Lonigan said she talked too much.

Marisol glanced back over her shoulder. Desirée's thick black hair was worn in one long, straight braid down her back. A red ribbon was threaded all through it; that had to take a lot of time to do every morning.

"So did you forget to get permission?" Marisol asked.

"No," Desirée said.

"Don't you want to go to ballet?"

"More than anything, more than anything in the world!" Desirée said. "But I can't." Her eyes became shiny with almost-tears.

Marisol stopped in the stairwell. "Why not?"

Desirée seemed to shrink into herself.

"Come on, why? Tell me. Hey, I've got a problem too."

Desirée was running her hand along the banister, looking everyplace except at Marisol. "Because—the clothing and ballet shoes."

"Your mom won't buy them for you?"

"She can't."

"Oh. Except for that—would she take you there?" Maybe, Marisol thought, maybe there was a chance for both of them!

"She can't."

"Because she's working, huh?" Marisol didn't know that shelter mothers worked; oh, snap, there went her bright idea. "Same with my dad. He won't take time off, either. I don't know what to do."

"No, because . . . she has to take my brothers. They're little; they have to come too."

"So what if they come with you?"

Desirée shrugged.

Why couldn't Desirée just *say* whatever it was! "Listen, tell me the problem with your brothers, because if you can get there, then maybe I could go along with you. I wouldn't bother anybody. I'd just walk alongside, just so I can tell my dad."

"I can't go," Desirée said.

"Why?"

"The subway tokens," she whispered. "I don't think Ti-Jean has to pay—he's the baby—but I, my mother, and Dieudonné . . . To go there and back again . . . *Mwen pa gen kob.*"

"What? What language is that?"

"Oh. I'm sorry. Creole. I didn't mean to . . ."

She had to be *really* upset, Marisol thought. Like Mrs. Garcia—when she got excited, she'd start speaking Spanish even if she was talking to an Anglo.

Marisol did some quick arithmetic in her head. "That's about ten dollars. Yeah, that's a lot. Can't you get someone to watch them, just for the afternoon?"

Desirée shook her head. "There is no one. And my mother, she would never leave them behind. She's afraid."

"What if—" Marisol was thinking fast. "What if my dad paid the fare? In exchange for you guys taking me along?" With her tokens added on, that would be . . . but Papi might . . .

"But the clothing . . ."

Marisol glanced at Desirée's jeans; they were loose on her and she wondered if they were charity. Shelter kids were really poor.

"You could dance in your jeans and socks," Marisol said.

Desirée fiercely shook her head.

Marisol grabbed her arm. "Let's go tell Mrs. Lonigan right now. If they're giving you a free scholarship, I bet they'd throw a leotard in!"

Desirée shook her head again.

"Come on!" Marisol tugged at her.

"We're supposed to go to the lunchroom."

"Hurry up, let's tell Mrs. Lonigan before she leaves!" So what if Gloria and Katie were saving a seat for her? So what if she was starving? This might work!

Desirée still pulled back.

"Come on, I'll do all the talking. All you have to do is stand there."

Some more tugs, and Marisol got Desirée to follow her up the stairs. It would be easy to tell Mrs. Lonigan about someone else's problem, Marisol thought; it was your own stuff that was hard to talk about. She could picture the school giving free leotards, tights, and ballet shoes to Desirée—they must have loads! But they sure wouldn't be sending a limo to Avenue C for her. Desirée was her only chance.

Desirée just stood there, clutching her hands together, while Marisol did all the talking. Mrs. Lonigan's expression went from very annoyed—"Why aren't you girls in lunch where you belong?"—to half sad, half uncomfortable in a flash. It was almost funny the way it changed so fast. And Mrs. Lonigan said right away that "arrangements" could be made. It was unfair, Marisol thought; just because Desirée was a shelter kid, she could get things for free. Papi had to work so hard for everything, six days a week and sometimes double shifts! But the way Desirée looked, as though she wanted the floor to open up and swallow her, and the way the teacher acted embarrassed and extra gentle with her, made Marisol glad she didn't have to beg for herself.

"Well, that's settled," Marisol told Desirée as they left the room. "Now all I have to do is ask Papi."

Desirée walked next to her without saying a word.

"Maybe I should've said something about the fare," Marisol continued. "Maybe Mrs. Lonigan could have made arrangements about that, too."

"I'm glad you didn't," Desirée said.

"Yeah, well, quit while you're ahead, right?"

"I'm sorry," Desirée said.

"About what? Hey, we're going to *dance!*"

A big wide smile broke out on Desirée's face.

Marisol couldn't keep herself from breaking into merengue steps right there in the hall. "*Coquí, coquí, el merengue del coquí,*" she sang.

Desirée swayed along with it. She was graceful, Marisol thought.

"Merengue." Desirée beamed. "From Haiti."

Marisol stopped. "No. *Coquí* is a little tree frog in Puerto Rico. Papi says you can hear them at night going '*coquí, coquí.*'"

"But the merengue is Haitian," Desirée said.

"No, it's Puerto Rican."

"Haitian," Desirée insisted.

"I'm *sure* from Puerto Rico," Marisol said. "I'll ask my dad." Where was Haiti, anyway?

They started down the stairs.

What if Papi wouldn't let her travel with a strange woman from the shelter? You could see some of them out on the street almost every day, buying crack with their babies right in their arms. Lots of people were homeless because of drugs and drinking, everybody knew that. But if Desirée's family had been burned out of their apartment, Papi might understand. Maybe that's what happened.

"How did you get to be in the shelter?" Marisol asked.

"There was no room in my father's cousin's apartment. That was in Brooklyn. There was no room. She had a new baby and her husband, he told us to go."

"What about before that?"

"We were in La Saline. In Port-au-Prince."

"Well, why did you leave there?"

"Before Father Aristide came back"—Desirée's voice dropped to a whisper—"there were the Tonton Macoutes with Uzis and machetes. They hurt my papa on rue Capois and he was very sick. The *houngan* couldn't make him get better."

That sounded like her father had died. Marisol wondered about *rue*, *tonton*, and *houngan*, but it didn't seem right to ask more questions.

There was a private party in the restaurant that night, so Papi wouldn't be coming home until late. Just when Marisol had something important to talk about!

Luis stuck a frozen pizza in the oven.

The smell of pepper and cheese made her mouth water. "I'm *starving*."

"Eyeballing the stove ain't gonna make it go any faster." He held out the bag of potato chips he'd brought from the Isla Verde. "Here."

She crunched a mouthful, a second mouthful, and then reluctantly handed back the bag.

"Keep it. I ate before."

"You did?" she said between chips.

"A piece of that barbecue *pollo* at Los Hermanos. Man, that's good."

"How come? What were you doing there?"

"You can't tell. Promise." He hesitated, but his eyes were sparkling—she could see he was itching to say something.

"I won't tell. What?"

"Tito treated me."

Her breath caught. "You hanging around him?"

"I ain't 'hanging around.' He was at Los Hermanos and he wanted me to get him beer from the Isla Verde. His special brand. Man, when Tito wants something, Mr. Rivera jumps—he said to forget about sweeping up and hurry up and go deliver it. So then Tito tells me to sit down and have some chicken, and we were sitting around talking."

"You shoulda gone right back to the store! Did he *make* you sit down?"

"Yeah, right." Luis laughed. "No, he's a good guy. We were talking, that's all. He likes me; he seen me hitting that triple last summer, that's how he knows me. We were talking regular stuff, like I was grown-up too."

"Papi says—"

"Papi worries too much," Luis said. "You oughtta know better than anybody."

"Yeah, but—"

"Guess what else. Tito keeps the apartment on B like for convenience, but he's got his *real* apartment on West End Avenue. He's got the whole Hudson outside his window. His woman is a model! He can get anything he wants. *Anything*. Like, snap, it's his."

"Nobody needs two apartments."

"He's smart. He's a cool guy."

"Luis—" Marisol's throat hurt. "Did he ask you to work for him?"

"Tito don't ask nobody to work for him. You want to work for him, you gotta do all the asking."

"You wouldn't, though. You wouldn't, right?"

"I'm not asking him nothing. He's interesting to talk to, that's all. . . . Hey, time's up, pizza's ready." Luis grabbed a pot holder and slid the pan out of the oven. He grinned. "Guess what, I'm starving too."

They cut the slices on the table. Marisol lifted one and it was too hot on her fingers. She caught the trailing strings of cheese on her tongue. She ate and kept her eyes on Luis.

He caught her look as he juggled his second slice. "The thing is, Papi trusts us so much. I can't go against that."

He took a big bite and Marisol watched him chewing.

"Papi's old-fashioned," he continued. "There's times I think I'm dumb, one hundred percent loco, to always be going by what he says."

"Papi tries so hard," Marisol said, "and he trusts us."

"I know," Luis said. "There's times I wish he didn't."

Finally Papi came home.

"Did you eat?" he asked.

"We made a pizza," Luis said.

"So you ain't hungry." Papi was smiling. "You're way too full for leftovers."

He emptied the bag he was carrying onto the table. There were stuffed mushrooms and pieces of melon with ham wrapped around them and chocolate-covered fresh strawberries. Luis and Marisol dove into them.

There was nothing in the world as good as a chocolate-covered strawberry, Marisol thought. "My most favorite thing!"

Luis was zipping through melon-and-ham pieces and collecting a pile of toothpicks in front of him. "What kind is this?"

"Prosciutto and casaba," Papi said.

"Great combo," Luis said.

"Expensive, too, so don't get used to it." Papi took a piece for himself. "The party worked out fine. Big tippers."

Papi was in a good mood, Marisol thought. Now was the best time. . . .

"Papi, about ballet—" she started.

He waved her away. "No more, I'm too tired for this. I told you—"

"Listen, Papi, I have someone to take me! This other girl in my class with a scholarship—remember, it was just the two of us? Well, she said I can go with her and her mom. Okay?"

"Her mother's taking you?"

"Uh-huh. So it works out fine, except for—"

"Who are they? Do we know the family?"

"No, but—"

"What's her name?"

"Desirée Joliecoeur. They're not Latino."

"I don't know them. Luis, do you?"

"No," Luis mumbled; he was still stuffing his face.

"Where do they live? Maybe I oughtta meet the mother. . . ."

"On Fourth Street. Papi! It's just a girl from my class and her mom!"

"I'll call her."

"You don't need to. Papi, Desirée is the most polite girl in the class, real quiet. I mean, she's *nice*." Marisol was picking her words carefully. Everything she was saying was true, so leaving a few things out wasn't lying. "They'll walk me home, right to the building, I promise. Papi, I want to go to ballet so bad! Say it's okay."

"I guess." Papi smiled. "It sounds all right."

"There's just one thing . . ." And Marisol told him about the carfare.

Papi frowned. "They don't have *anything*?"

"The father died, so they're having hard times."

Papi nodded; he understood about hard times.

"Please," Marisol said. "It's my chance."

She knew Papi was thinking: twelve dollars every week. There was nothing more she could say or do. She held her breath and waited. It felt like forever.

"I want you to have this chance," Papi said. He sounded very serious. "Use it well, Marisol."

"Thank you!" She jumped up and hugged him with all her strength. "I'm so happy! I'm gonna dance and dance and dance!"

Papi picked her up and twirled her around and around, and the refrigerator and the table and Luis spun by in a big, happy blur.

She couldn't fall asleep that night.

"Luis," she whispered. "I don't know how to dance ballet. What if everybody else—"

"It's bad enough I got to split a room with you," he muttered. "At least shut up and let me sleep."

Long after Luis was breathing slowly and deeply in his bed, Marisol was still wide awake and thinking.

What would class be like? What about the other kids? She didn't know her way around uptown. And Desirée's mom . . . Papi never suspected that she wasn't telling him the whole truth. She hoped Desirée's mom would turn out to be a regular mother.

Marisol waited in front of her building. She took the note out of her pocket and read the instructions from the school again. "Capezio, 1650 Broadway at Fifty-first Street. Black leotard, pink footed tights, pink kid slippers—elastic, no ribbon." Marisol had a lot of money and it made her feel anxious. She had divided it up, just in case—some in her jeans, some in her jacket, some in her shoe. Desirée had a voucher—but where was she?

Sunlight flitted in and out of the clouds. Marisol stuck her hands in her pockets. She felt the note under her fingers. Capezio, she thought. It was a store for dance things and even the name sounded special. She was too excited to be standing still.

There was no sign of them on the avenue. They'd said three-thirty. They were late. Maybe Haitian time was like Puerto Rican time. What if they were late next week, too, when ballet class started? That would be awful!

She watched Johnny Castro coming along the sidewalk. He'd become awfully thin; he looked bad. His walk was twitchy. Johnny lived on the third floor with his grandmother. He'd always been nice to her; he'd played with her when she was little. He taught her how to do "around the world" with a yo-yo. He used to call her mi gatita, my little kitten. But she was too conscious of all that money in her pockets. Johnny wouldn't take anything, not from her—anyway, he had plenty of money working for Tito—but he was a junkie now, so you never knew. He stopped in front of the door. "Hey, Marisol, ¿qué pasa?" He smiled and looked in her direction, but his eyes were darting all over the place.

"Hey, Johnny." She wanted to tell that she was going for ballet shoes! But she didn't say anything.

He had grown a mustache and his round baby face had turned angular, but he had that same good-natured smile. It was confusing; Marisol couldn't, just snap, stop liking Johnny Castro, but she hated junkies.

"Nothing happening, huh?" he said. He was jumpy; his foot was tapping.

"I'm getting dance lessons," she said.

"Uh-huh, good, good," he said.

The old Johnny Castro would have asked about it; he would have been excited with her.

She watched him start upstairs. He clinked his ring against the banister in a weird rhythm of his own.

She looked down the street again. Where were they?

And then she saw them inching their way toward her. Desirée's mother was holding a baby in one arm and a big paper shopping bag in the other. The baby was struggling to get down, so she let him go and he was barely toddling along, hanging on to her hand. Desirée had the other kid by the hand, but he was pulling away and reaching for his mother. So then Desirée took the shopping bag and the mother picked up the baby again and held on to the other kid.

Desirée waved as they came closer. The mother had a mostly red, flowered kerchief wound around her hair. She was wearing a violet quilted parka and a black-and-white striped skirt that didn't match anything. She was skinny and coffee-colored, like Desirée. The baby's big eyes contrasted with his very dark skin as he peered at Marisol from his mother's shoulder. The other kid looked about five; he stared at Marisol with his thumb in his mouth.

"This is my mother and Dieudonné, everyone calls him Donny, and the baby's Ti-Jean," Desirée said.

Mrs. Joliecoeur looked tired and hassled. She said something in that other language, Creole.

"My mother, she says sorry we're late," Desirée translated. "Were you waiting long?"

Marisol shrugged. "I came downstairs early." She hesitated. "Doesn't your mom speak English?"

Desirée shook her head. "You know what happened?" She shifted the shopping bag to her other hand. "We had the baby dressed, but after we got Donny ready, then the baby, he needed a change, so that's why."

"Oh."

"Dieudonné, say hello to my friend."

They weren't exactly friends, Marisol thought.

The little boy's thumb popped out. "H'lo."

He had a clip-on bow tie. And Desirée had changed from her school clothes. She was wearing a dress under her jacket; it was a faded red, but it looked starched enough to stand up by itself. Her long braid was wound around in a bun on top of her head, festooned with red and pink ribbons. Marisol was in her jeans, and she'd been so anxious to get going that she'd hardly washed up after school.

Marisol thought she ought to say something to Mrs. Jolieceour, to be polite. "Uh—tell your mother, thanks a lot for taking me."

Desirée spoke in Creole.

Mrs. Jolieceour smiled at Marisol and said, "Hel-lo." There was a missing tooth on the side, but she had a great smile, the kind that makes you smile back right away.

"I guess we oughtta get started," Marisol said.

"We go to East Houston?" Desirée asked.

"Right." Second Avenue, off East Houston, was the closest subway stop.

"And we go uptown," Desirée said.

"Yeah," Marisol said. "We have to change trains someplace to get to the Broadway line."

Desirée and her mother spoke in Creole. Mrs. Joliecouer looked worried.

"Uh—doesn't your mother know the way?"

Desirée shook her head.

Oh, man, Marisol thought, Papi wouldn't like this one bit. "We'll look at the subway map," she said. "We'll figure it out."

"I don't wanta go!" Donny burst out.

Desirée pulled him along as they straggled up the street.

Marisol started worrying that the store might close before they ever got there.

There weren't enough seats together on the F train. Mrs. Joliecoeur sat stiffly, on guard, with the baby on her lap and Donny next to her. Marisol saw two empty seats at the other end of the car; she rushed over and saved one for Desirée. But Mrs. Joliecouer waved them back; she wanted them to stay close. That made no sense, Marisol thought; even Papi let her sit anyplace she wanted as long as he could see her. And the car was full of regular people just going about their business. But Desirée didn't argue at all, so they went back and held on to a nearby pole and swayed with the train.

They got off at Forty-second Street. That's where they had to change to the Seven to get to the Broadway line; Marisol had seen that on the subway map. But they didn't know where to find the Seven. When Marisol asked a lady for directions, she gave them a quick look and brushed right by, as if she thought they wanted something from her. That made Marisol mad! The next lady was nice; she explained how to go and pointed the way. They had to go up one flight of stairs and down another, to a whole different platform. The Seven took them to Times Square. When they were finally going uptown on the One local, with only one stop to go, Marisol felt proud and happy; they'd come all this way without getting a bit lost!

They came out of the subway on Broadway and Fiftieth Street. The sky was all clouds now. The big movie marquees looked shabby in the gray light.

Marisol checked the note again. "It says 1650 Broadway, at Fifty-first Street."

They walked toward Fifty-first Street and checked the numbers on the buildings. All even numbers.

"1650's even, right?" Marisol asked. She was never sure when the number ended with a zero.

"I think so," Desirée said.

There was the Winter Garden Theater and then, where 1650 should have been, nothing but a big blank wall.

They walked up to Fifty-second Street, but the numbers were getting too high.

"It *says* Fifty-first Street." Marisol frowned. "Maybe it's really an odd number."

They crossed Broadway. It wasn't easy, with cabs making quick turns even when they didn't have the right of way. Marisol helped hold on to Donny.

The building numbers were 1647, 1649, 1651. . . .

They stopped and formed a knot in the middle of the sidewalk. Other people rushed around them. *"M pa we-l."* Desirée and her mother were talking in Creole. Dieudonné tried to run in a circle around them and Mrs. Joliecoeur kept pulling him close. She looked upset.

"My mother, she says we're in the wrong place."

"But it says right here . . ." Marisol insisted. Luis and Papi could've found it in a minute, Marisol thought.

Desirée looked embarrassed. "My mother, she's sorry. . . ."

"It has to be on the other side!" Marisol glanced back across the street, frustrated, and then she saw it: CAPEZIO, written in big script across the second-floor windows over the blank wall. "Look, there!"

They waited for the light and recrossed Broadway, working their way around a stopped bus and through exhaust fumes. Donny dragged his feet. The baby started whimpering. "Ti-Jean, dous, dous Ti-Jean," Mrs. Joliecoeur crooned to him.

"There's no door," Desirée said.

Marisol stared at the blank wall. She craned her neck and looked up at the second floor. "But it's up there."

They followed the wall around the corner. Halfway to Seventh Avenue, they finally found an entrance: 1650!

"That's not right," Marisol said. "It's not on Broadway at all, it's on Fifty-first Street. But hey, we made it!"

When they stepped out of the elevator on the second floor, the first thing Marisol saw was a mannequin of a dancer—well, not a mannequin, it wasn't like a store dummy—oh, snap, she didn't know *what* to call it. It was big and in a dancer's pose and it was made entirely of faded pink-beige ballet shoes! Their ribbons were dangling everywhere, giving it a fuzzy outline. Marisol wanted to touch, just very gently. . . .

To the right there was a counter with a sign that said MAKEUP CENTER. That had to be stage makeup for dancers. Marisol wished she could see, but none was out on display. A lady was folding a pile of T-shirts with a leaping silhouette and *Alvin Ailey* in bold writing on them. What was Alvin Ailey?

Another step and there was a stand hung with cloth bags in different sizes, something like school bags but . . .

"Oh, I know! They're *ballet* bags," Marisol breathed, "to carry your stuff in!" There was a bunch of small pink ones. She liked those best. She ran her finger along a shoulder strap.

"All for dancing." Desirée sounded awed.

"Come on, let's see everything," Marisol said.

They moved into a wide-open space. The store covered a whole city block, all the way from Broadway to Seventh Avenue. One long side had floor-to-ceiling windows. They walked to the right, along an endless wall with packages of tights in a million colors. Footless. Sparkling. Ankle. Fishnet.

"I like sparkling," Marisol said.

Mrs. Joliecoeur followed behind them, keeping a tight grip on Donny's arm; he was trying to wriggle loose.

Small signs said PLEASE ASK FOR SERVICE.

"Dieudonné! Don't touch!" Desirée was bossy with him.

Bodysuits, leotards, sweatpants, and T-shirts hung on racks along the window side.

They retraced their steps, back past the makeup center, and went all the way to the left where it said SHOE DEPARTMENT. And that was the best part: a wall full of little glass shelves and each shelf had a different kind of shoe on it. Marisol read the labels. Men's Character. Jazz Boot. Moonlight Ballroom. Split-Sole. Jazz Tap. Ballroom Silver. The names alone were magical! A high-heeled shoe was all gold sparkles. A red satin ballet slipper had shiny matching ribbons streaming from it.

A salesman was waiting close by, near a row of chairs. Marisol was glad he didn't interrupt their looking. She wanted to study every single shoe and figure out what everything meant. But when Mrs. Joliecoeur sat down, with the baby and a bottle, and Dieudonné, and her lumpy paper shopping bag, the salesman approached them. He said something to Mrs. Joliecoeur and she shook her head helplessly; Desirée rushed right over and Marisol followed.

"We need ballet shoes, please," Desirée said.

"For the two of us," Marisol added.

He smiled. "Well, you're in the right place." Marisol was glad that he was young and not snotty. "What kind?"

Marisol pulled the note out of her pocket anyway, though she had memorized it. "Pink kid slippers. Elastic, no ribbon," she read off. She hesitated. "I like the ribbons, though."

"You're beginners?" he asked.

"Uh-huh."

"The elastic band is better to start with. Holds the shoe to your foot nicely; it's much harder to get ribbons tied just right. What school?"

"Manhattan Ballet School," Marisol said.

"Oh, that's the best," he said. "Top-notch."

Marisol felt a warm glow.

"Okay, I know exactly what they want," he continued. "Pink, full sole. Let's check your sizes."

Marisol and Desirée bent over to unlace their sneakers.

"I kind of want the red satin," Marisol said.

He laughed. "So would I," he said, "but Manhattan's Level One is pink slippers, pink tights, black leotard. That's the way it is."

Marisol was glad she'd remembered to put on new socks. She glanced at Desirée's; they were clean, no holes, but the heels were worn thin.

"Take your socks off, girls. I'll get you some try-on peds."

He went to the back.

"What are 'peds'?" Desirée whispered.

"Those thin nylon things that just cover your foot," Marisol answered.

Mrs. Joliecoeur asked something and Desirée answered.

When the salesman returned, they slipped on the peds and stood up to be measured.

"I take size five," Marisol said.

"You go down about two sizes for ballet shoes," he said.

And then he brought out the boxes and there they were, pale pink nestled between layers of tissue! Marisol's breath caught. She put hers on and couldn't stop staring at her feet.

Mrs. Joliecoeur was speaking urgently to Desirée.

"My mother, she says I should wear them with my socks."

He looked at Desirée, puzzled.

Her eyes were on the ground. "So when my feet grow . . ."

Marisol listened carefully. She'd promised Papi they'd last her for a long time.

The salesman shook his head. "Ballet slippers have to fit like a *glove.*" He looked at Desirée kindly. "They really do. Tell your mother it's absolutely necessary."

There was a conference between Desirée and her mother, and Mrs. Joliecoeur nodded.

The elastic bands came separately in the box. The salesman showed them how to fold the slippers over. "Where they break, that's where you sew the elastic on each side. Okay?"

Later they got leotards and tights too, and Desirée handed over her voucher and Marisol took the money out of all her pockets, but from then on she was floating in a dream. She had *ballet shoes!*

At the elevator, Desirée said, "My mother, she says she'll take your shoes and sew the elastic on for you."

Marisol hadn't even thought about how she'd manage to do that. But she clutched her box tight; she wasn't ready to give them up even for a moment.

"Don't worry," Desirée said. "My mother, she does fine stitching. She sewed for the rich ladies in Pétionville."

"It's not that," Marisol said. "Tell your mom thanks a lot. That's real nice of her. I can't sew for anything, and Papi sure can't!"

Marisol smiled her thank-you and Mrs. Joliecoeur smiled back. She *was* nice.

"I'll bring them to school for you tomorrow, I promise," Desirée said.

"Okay."

Marisol wasn't about to hand them over until the very last minute. She held on to her Capezio shopping bag.

The subway car was full of people coming home from work. We look like a ragtag group, Marisol thought, and that's the truth. The baby had spit up on Mrs. Joliecoeur's shoulder and there was a sour smell all around them. Donny was acting up and Marisol couldn't blame him; he'd had a whole afternoon of nothing but being reined in. And Mrs. Joliecoeur with her hassled expression and unmatched clothing sure didn't look like a regular person coming from a job.

Marisol smoothed out the side of the plastic bag so that the "Capezio" showed up bright and clear. That way, everyone on the subway would know she was a dancer.

11

At school, Marisol hung out with Gloria, Katie, and Linda. They used to call themselves the Fresh Four, but by the time they reached fifth grade, fresh was played out; no one would say that except on TV sitcoms. They became the Fab Four. They always stayed together at recess and they saved seats for each other at lunch.

Marisol thought maybe she was supposed to be friendlier to Desirée now—but the truth was, she wouldn't fit in with the Fab Four. They talked fast and loud and had a million things to say to each other. . . .

But when Desirée gave Marisol her ballet shoes in the morning, they had a moment together. Marisol opened the box, unfolded the tissue paper, and gently touched the pale-pink leather.

The elastic bands were attached with tiny, absolutely even stitches. "Thanks, that's so perfect," Marisol said.

"See—my mother, she sewed a double row."

Marisol ran her finger along the stitches. "I can't hardly even feel them. Tell her thanks a *lot*."

"So we're all ready to start." Desirée took a deep

breath. "Next Wednesday." She sounded scared.

"Next Wednesday." There was a little flutter starting in Marisol's stomach. "Hey, listen. They picked us, didn't they? So we belong there." Even if it *was* uptown, Marisol thought. "It's gonna be wonderful!"

Desirée smiled, that big sudden light-up smile just like her mother's.

Marisol put the shoe box on her desk. She pointed at it when she caught Gloria's eye across the room. Gloria shrugged, puzzled.

"My ballet slippers," Marisol mouthed.

Gloria shook her head. "What?" she mouthed back.

"Ballet slippers," Marisol was mouthing slowly when Mrs. Lonigan's voice cut across the room. "Marisol! Eyes front!"

So she tried to concentrate on the numbers that Mrs. Lonigan was scribbling on the board, but she couldn't resist sneaking her hand under the lid a couple of times.

Marisol took the shoe box to lunch and planted it in the middle of the cafeteria table. She drew back the tissue to show Gloria, Katie, and Linda. "*Mira,* aren't they beautiful?" she breathed.

"I useta have pink sneakers," Linda said, "but they got dirty in a minute."

Marisol held one slipper up on her hand. "Look at it, look how beautiful."

"Uh-huh, they're nice," Gloria said. "I hate peanut butter; who wants to trade?"

Linda crumpled her brown paper bag. "I'll trade you half an American cheese."

They were passing sandwiches right over her slippers! And with tomato dripping out of Linda's! Marisol protectively covered the box with her hands.

"You got any soda?" Katie tossed her milk carton to Gloria.

"Hey, look out!" Marisol yelled.

"What?"

"You could've spilled that on my slippers!"

"So get them out of the way," Gloria said.

"But I was showing you—"

"We saw them," Katie said. She frowned at the school lunch on her tray. "They always have macaroni."

"That's why I bring from home," Gloria said, "but I told my mom no more peanut butter, and look what she gave me."

"Hey, Marisol, you better go get your lunch," Katie said. "They're down to the end of the line."

Marisol closed the lid and reluctantly put the shoe box on her chair. "Watch my shoes, all right?"

"Okay," Gloria said.

"Don't let anybody touch them. Make sure nobody—"

"Okay, okay. You're making such a big deal out of it," Gloria said. "Oh—what were you trying to tell me before? In class?"

"I forgot," Marisol said. "Nothing."

The whole week went like that. Marisol did all the

regular things: school, early mass on Sunday before Papi left for work, the after-school program where the crafts lady was teaching knitting; Gloria liked that and Marisol went along with her. And all through everything, ballet class was in the back of Marisol's mind. Gloria didn't act mad anymore about not being chosen; that was ancient history. She just didn't seem the least bit interested. So Marisol didn't talk much about it with the Fab Four.

She got Papi to hammer a nail into the wall over her bed, under the picture of the Virgin Mary. She hung the ballet slippers from it. They were the last thing she saw when she went to sleep and the first thing she saw when she woke up in the morning.

Luis thought it was dumb. "Hang *all* your shoes up on the wall, why don'tcha? Hang up your underwear too."

"Why don'tcha shut up?" Marisol snapped.

Nobody understood.

The only time she had a chance to share her excitement was when she passed Desirée's desk in the classroom.

"Five more days to go," Marisol whispered, and Desirée's eyes sparkled.

Then it was "three more days to go."

And, finally, "one more day," and they gave each other high fives.

On Wednesday, Marisol ran home from school. She washed up extra carefully. She brushed her teeth. Then she pulled on the pink tights and the black leotard. She and Desirée had talked about that a lot; they'd decided to wear them under their clothes, because there might not be a place to change at ballet school.

Marisol studied herself in the full-length mirror in back of the closet door. She stood on her toes. She turned and stared at her profile. The mirror was wavy in the middle and her reflection was unreal, shimmering in front of her. She felt almost dizzy, as if she were standing at the very edge of something. As if she might never be the same again.

Marisol was glad the Joliecoeurs came on time. Desirée's braid was wound around on top of her head with a million pink ribbons; it looked pretty. Her jacket's zipper was open and Marisol could see a little cloth packet hanging from a string around her neck.

"What's that?" Marisol asked.

"A wanga."

"A what?"

"My mother, she wanted me to wear it. For good luck. It's like a charm."

"Oh."

Maybe good luck put the ballet school on the same subway line as Capezio, so they pretty much knew the way from Times Square. They caught an express—that was lucky too, because they didn't have much time.

But then the train went right by the Lincoln Center station! It was awful for Marisol to look out the window and see them speeding past it; for a moment, she felt panicked. They got off at Seventy-second Street and had to walk six blocks downtown. Mrs. Joliecoeur shifted the baby to her other arm. Desirée pulled Donny along. They were going so slow! On her own, Marisol would have been running or maybe skipping. Okay, she'd know for next time; Lincoln Center was a local stop.

At Sixty-sixth Street, Broadway met Columbus Avenue, so there were two big streets at once with cars going in all directions. It was hard to cross, even with the traffic lights. Marisol helped hold on to Donny.

Then they were at Lincoln Center. Marisol looked all around at the big white buildings and the plaza and the restaurants and a big fountain—it was beautiful!—and colorful banners that announced OPERA and NEW YORK PHILHARMONIC. She would have liked to see more, but they had to hurry down another block, to Amsterdam Avenue. Finally they found the school. At least the entrance was where it was supposed to be.

They squeezed into a crowded elevator with creaky iron gates—well, the five of them coming in sure made a crowd! There were two teenage girls and both of them had their hair up in buns high on their heads. Marisol thought they were beautiful; they had to be real dancers! There was a little white girl holding hands with a black lady in a uniform. On the way up, Marisol could hear snatches of music coming from other floors. She took everything in, looking and listening.

On the third floor, there was a lobby with wooden benches where Mrs. Joliecoeur could sit.

"Oh, good," Desirée said. "My mother, she was so worried about where she'd wait."

The black lady in the uniform sat down there too.

A receptionist behind a desk pointed Marisol and Desirée toward the dressing room. It was at the end of a long hallway with different rooms coming off it. Studio One, Studio Two, Studio Three.

The first two were big empty rooms with pale wooden floors and mirrored walls. The door of the third was closed, but Marisol could hear piano music and the faint thump of feet.

They heard the voices coming from the dressing room before they entered. It was full of girls talking, giggling, some undressed, some putting on ballet shoes. Piles of clothing covered the benches that ran around the room. Marisol and Desirée had to separate to find empty spots.

Marisol folded her jeans, sweater, and jacket and tucked them behind her on the bench as she sat down. She took her ballet slippers out of the Capezio bag. Lots of the girls had cloth ballet bags like she'd seen at the store. Some of girls had lacy underwear, brand-new, bright white. One of the girls wore a bra, though she had nothing at all to fill it! As Marisol put on her slippers, she glanced at the girl next to her. She was a cute, freckled redhead.

"Do we get lockers or something?" Marisol asked.

"No," the girl said. "Everyone leaves their things here."

"Oh." Maybe uptown kids didn't have to worry about someone stealing their stuff.

"It looks like a big class," the redhead said. "Looks like there's fifteen of us."

"Have you gone here before?" Marisol asked.

"No, we're all Level One. Black-leotard beginners." The redhead glanced around the room. "I bet that's the scholarship kid." She was indicating Desirée.

Marisol stiffened.

"They take a couple of inner-city kids every year," she continued.

Marisol's face felt hot. "I'm scholarship too. So what? I had to try *out* and I got *picked*—"

"I didn't mean anything . . ."

"—because I was the *best*!"

"I said I didn't mean anything. You don't have to bite my head off."

"And we don't live in some *inner* city!"

"I swear, you've got a temper bad as mine," the redhead said. "Want to start over? My name's Claire, what's yours?"

"Marisol. Marisol Perez."

"Marisol. That's a pretty name."

"Thanks," Marisol muttered. She felt stupid for flaring up. She hesitated and then, "Claire's a nice name too."

"No, it's not." Claire wrinkled her nose. "It's as plain as anything."

They both smiled a little.

"Come on, let's go. Madame has a fit if someone's late."

"How do you know all this stuff?"

"Because my big sister takes classes here. And by the way, *everybody* has to audition. There's dozens and dozens of girls auditioning for every single place. So *everybody* here is the best."

"Oh." Marisol felt her confidence draining down to the floor.

Claire grinned. "Scary, isn't it?"

Marisol was surprised; in leotard and tights, Desirée was slim-hipped and amazingly long-legged. Marisol realized that Desirée's regular clothes were mostly too big for her; that's why she looked so different now.

Marisol and Desirée kept close to each other—for just a second, they clutched hands—as everyone filed into Studio Two. Fifteen girls with different hair colors and faces became somehow identical in the uniform of black leotards, pink tights, and pink slippers. Blending in made Marisol feel more confident. She'd just watch and do like everybody else.

The first thing was a box near the door with white powder in it. One of the girls stepped into it and Marisol and Desirée were about to follow along.

"Don't, we're not supposed to," Claire said. "That's for when we're on toe."

They'd be on toe! Marisol hoped it would be soon—maybe today!

"What is it?" she asked.

"Rosin," Claire said, "so your shoes won't slip."

"Oh." Okay, rosin. She'd remember that.

One wall was all mirrored and the opposite wall had long windows. The bare wood floor shone. There was a piano on the side and a man was sitting on the piano bench. The lady from tryouts was in the center of the room. She was exactly the way Marisol had remembered her over and over again—jet-black hair in a topknot, skin like ivory, and a black skirt that fluttered when she moved. She was holding some kind of very thin stick. Marisol wondered what it was for. A magic wand? There was something magical about her.

"So—a new batch of little swans. I am Madame Gourenev. You may call me Madame." She clapped her hands. "To the barre, please."

Say what? Marisol thought.

The other girls scurried to line up in front of a pole that ran the length of the room in front of the mirror. It was a little more than waist high. Marisol and Desirée made sure to find places next to each other.

Madame walked along the line of girls, studying them with her huge dark eyes. Her feet, in black ballet shoes, seemed to be skimming the floor. Her back was ramrod straight. She walked like a queen, Marisol thought.

"Your hair should be neatly pulled back," Madame said. "I must see clear faces. Next time, everyone please be prepared."

A girl with long brown waves over her cheeks tried to knot her hair, but it kept tumbling loose. Most of the girls had buns or ponytails. Why did the Fab Four ever decide a shag cut was cool? Marisol wondered. What was she going to do with all the little wisps?

"So—now we begin," Madame said. "Spread out, ladies. Yes, that's good."

Marisol was almost quivering with anticipation. Finally, the beginning, right now! Her attention was riveted on Madame.

"Hands on the barre. Stand close enough to keep your hand on it slightly in front of you. If you have to reach for it, you're pulled off center. Too close makes your shoulders hunch."

Marisol adjusted.

"Seat under, stomach up, so your back is straight and flat. Lift up your ribs so your chest feels high. Chin up."

Marisol looked at Desirée in front of her. The scoop neck of the leotard and the braid wound high on Desirée's head emphasized a long, graceful neck—and for once, Desirée was holding her head up.

"Weight forward over the balls of your feet. Lift yourself up, up out of your hips so your body feels long."

Everything about Desirée was long. Marisol sneaked a glance at herself in the mirror.

"You—pull up your thigh muscles so your knees are very straight."

Who was she talking to? Marisol tensed her thigh muscles until they hurt.

"Imagine a line that starts at the crown of your head and goes straight down your middle, ending between your feet. This is your axis."

It was a posture lesson, Marisol thought. What was this, anyway? When were they going to *dance*?

And then she found out what the magic wand was for. It wasn't so magic, after all. Madame used it to make corrections as she walked along the line of girls. "Keep your hips even and straight," and when she came to Marisol, a tap on her shoulder and, "No, no, shoulder blades down, don't force them back."

Madame never raised her voice, but the *no, no*'s felt like the crack of a whip.

Then Madame showed them the five positions. "Everything in ballet starts from the five positions," she said. "That is your base."

Madame's feet moved from position to position fluidly, as if they had a life of their own.

The first position was heels touching and feet turned out. "A straight line from the toes of your right foot to the toes of your left foot," Madame said. "You see."

Madame made it look easy, but then she said, "No, no, no! The turnout must come from the hips. Open your legs outward only as far as your hips will allow." And it wasn't that easy.

Madame stopped in front of Desirée. "You can't have a necklace bouncing against your chest. Please remove it."

Desirée, flustered, fumbled with the string of the

wanga. She put it on the floor next to the wall. When she stood up again, her shoulders were curled inward. Marisol felt bad for her, but at least Madame had called it a necklace.

"Head high and proud," Madame told her.

Up close, Marisol could see little lines in the skin around Madame's eyes. Her black eyeliner extended way past the corners and her lashes were incredibly long.

In third position, the heel of Marisol's right foot had to be in front of the arch of the left foot.

"Right foot!" For a moment, in a panic, Marisol didn't know her right from her left. She switched and quickly switched back; she'd been right the first time.

"Seats tucked under," Madame reminded with little taps of the wand on backsides.

There was so much to think about all at once. And none of it was anything like dancing.

The fifth position was the hardest: the heel of the right foot in front of the big toe of the left foot and then turned back so both feet were touching at all points. Marisol couldn't do it all the way, but she tried hard; she wanted to be the best.

"No, no! Don't force it," Madame said to her.

They turned to do the five positions over again with the left foot. "The outside foot. Always the outside foot!" And Madame kept talking about "turnout." "You cannot achieve full turnout immediately. It will come only with hard work," and "No, no, no! Turn out from the hips, only from the hips!" and "You! Keep yourself centered."

Marisol didn't know which "you" she meant. She hoped it wasn't her.

Madame nodded to the pianist. Live piano music just for them! Maybe now the dancing would start. . . .

"Port de bras," Madame said. That turned out to mean the positions of the arms and you had to move them exactly the way she said, to the count. And sometimes you were supposed to turn your head toward your hand and sometimes you were supposed to keep your head facing front. Marisol watched to see what Desirée, in front of her, was doing.

"You! Elbow up!"

Her elbow *was* up, Marisol thought. Whew, she meant somebody else.

"Raise arm—and one. Open to side—and two. . . ."

The piano music was melodic and peaceful. Marisol let her arm float with the rhythm. . . .

Oh, snap, this time the tap of the wand was for her, a touch raising her hand. "Don't break at the wrist. Hand in line with the arm."

Marisol looked at Madame.

"No, no, head front."

Maybe that's what Jeanne Carlsen meant when she said ballet took a lot of discipline. And the truth was, Marisol thought, she didn't have discipline; she felt like breaking out and dancing salsa. Was this all there was to ballet? Disappointment was a knot in her chest.

"When do we go on toe?" she whispered to the girl behind her.

"Third year, red leotards," the girl whispered back.

"Oh."

Madame looked hard at her and clapped her hands. She'd only said a couple of words, Marisol thought. Madame was worse than Mrs. Lonigan!

They learned demi-pliés. They faced the barre and held it with both hands and bent their knees partway.

"Bend your knees to count—and one and two," Madame said. "Straighten to count—and three and four."

They did it in first and second positions.

"Heels on floor—and one and two."

They did it over and over again, and Marisol was thinking she'd gone to an awful lot of trouble to get here and this wasn't what she had expected. . . . But anyway, she wanted to be the best. She hoped Madame was noticing how straight she kept her back.

Grand plié was deep bends, four slow counts to bend, four slow counts to straighten. This time they were allowed to lift their heels.

"Grand plié—one and two and three and four . . ."

Desirée turned to Marisol, beaming. "Everything's in French!"

"You understand all that? Is French like Creole?" Marisol asked.

"You! No talking!" Madame said. More discipline! "And one and two and three and . . .

"Dancers do pliés every day of their lives. The muscles of the legs must be elastic," Madame said.

There were battements tendus with port de bras, eight times with the right foot and then they turned around and did eight with the left foot. Now a blond girl was in front of Marisol. She watched her and tried to do everything right and hoped the next "No, no, no!" wouldn't be for her. *Battements, ronds de jambe, relevés* —so many words to remember. Desirée was lucky she understood French.

When the barre work was over, Madame had them come to the center of the floor. More exercises, more things to remember, and no barre to lean on for balance. And stretches on the floor until Marisol was feeling muscles she never knew she had. One was with legs together, straight out on the floor in front, toes pointed; they were supposed to bend their whole bodies over their legs and make their chests touch their knees. Marisol couldn't get her body down that far. No way! Someone groaned out loud.

"Ah yes, but if you do this," Madame said, "then perhaps one day you will do *this*."

Madame slowly extended her right leg backward, very slowly, amazingly higher and higher. She swept her arms backward and held the position, looking like a bird about to soar. Then she bent her body forward to the toe remaining on the ground. She held the pose in motionless beauty for breathtaking moments, a long straight line from the foot pointed high in the air to the long length of neck near the floor.

Marisol didn't know she was holding her breath until someone's whispered *arabesque* broke the spell.

As Madame slowly straightened, her feet floated together into fifth position. "Continue, like rubber bands, down—and one and two, up—and three and four. . . ."

Marisol willed her body to bend, just a little farther. She'd *make* her muscles turn elastic, she would!

Then their hour was up.

"Very nice, ladies." Madame smiled for the first time that afternoon. "When you get home, soak in a hot bath, perhaps with Epsom salts. I don't want my little swans to be aching tomorrow."

The very last thing before they were dismissed was the reverence.

"At the end of class, it's good manners to thank Mr. Easton for playing for you and to thank me. Raise your right arm forward toward Mr. Easton and place one foot behind the other. Make a good firm platform with your toes. Slowly bend the knee that you are standing on."

It's only a curtsy, Marisol thought, but there was a very particular way to do it. There was a very particular way to do everything in ballet.

"Keeping your back very straight will help you balance. Slowly straighten up again."

Marisol bent her knee as far as she could—she wanted to do the lowest reverence of anybody—but she was wobbling. She checked her reflection in the mirror. ¡*Ay, Dios mio!* She didn't look anything like Madame! She quickly rounded her arm, remembering the port de bras.

"Now with your other foot and arm, toward me," Madame said.

Marisol liked ending the class in this special way. The formal ritual set it apart from the everyday world, the way church on Sundays was a hushed space separate from the noisy street outside.

As they filed out, Marisol passed close to Madame. She noticed that the porcelain-white color of her skin stopped at the base of her neck. Her collarbone jutted out. The scooped leotard showed freckles on her chest where the makeup had ended. Madame wasn't that young. She wasn't really beautiful. It didn't matter. She could make her body move in superhuman ways, with heart-stopping absolute perfection. And Marisol was sure, more sure than she'd ever been of anything in her whole life, that she wanted to become exactly like her.

13

The dressing room smelled of sweat and perfume. Marisol zipped up her jeans. Her tights and leotard felt damp underneath. She was sorry she hadn't brought underwear along. Lots of the girls came in wearing leotards, but they had something to change into after class. Well, she and Desirée would know for next time.

Claire was brushing her hair next to Marisol.

"How does Madame do that—what-do-you-call-it—arabesque? Wasn't that awesome?" Marisol said.

"Oh, she's good. She used to be with the Bolshoi; she even danced *Giselle* with Nureyev."

What did all that mean? Marisol bit her lip. There was so much she didn't know about!

She didn't want to sound stupid, but curiosity finally got to her. "Bolshoi?"

"The Russian ballet," Claire said.

"Oh . . . Is Madame Russian?"

"Of course."

Then why does she speak in French? Marisol thought. The ballet world was full of mysteries.

As she and Desirée were leaving, one of the girls pulled off her ballet shoes and shoved them carelessly into her Capezio bag. "I hate this! My mother's *making* me come," she complained. "It's so boring!"

It wasn't fair! That girl had it so easy and Marisol had to worry about whether Mrs. Joliecoeur would keep on taking them. Because when they got to the waiting room, the baby was howling and Mrs. Joliecoeur was frantically shushing him. Everyone stared at them. Donny was squirming and whining. Mrs. Joliecoeur looked exhausted. She said something to Desirée that didn't sound like good news.

"Is your mom mad?" Marisol asked.

"No, but it's too hard to wait and keep them quiet. Dieudonné, with nothing to do. And Ti-Jean—"

"Uh—isn't there anyplace they could go, while we—"

Desirée shook her head.

"Donny's good," Desirée said defensively, "but he's only a little boy."

The subway car was crowded; there were no empty seats. Mrs. Joliecoeur leaned against a pole with the baby hanging over her shoulder, finally asleep. Donny kicked his legs restlessly while Desirée kept a tight grip on his arm.

"Do you think . . ." Marisol was almost afraid to find out. "You think your mother will take us again next week?"

"Oh, yes! I *want* to go. And she wants this for me. Very much."

"Your mom's great, I mean it!" Marisol looked at Mrs.

Joliecoeur. "Somebody ought to give her a seat." Then she raised her voice, real loud. "Somebody ought to give a lady with a baby a seat!"

A lot of people looked away, but finally a woman got up for her. Mrs. Joliecoeur smiled and nodded as she gratefully sank down. She adjusted Ti-Jean on her lap; he didn't wake up at all.

"You're so brave," Desirée whispered. "You can say anything!"

"There's no law says you can't," Marisol said. "There's nothing to be scared of."

"Except Madame."

"And her magic wand," Marisol added.

"Is that what it's called?"

"No, I made that up. Because she's like a queen in a fairy tale."

"A very strict queen but not *mean*. Not the kind that gives you a poison apple," Desirée said.

"No. A *queenly* queen." Marisol smiled. "Isn't she *wonderful?*"

Marisol put her heels together in first position and Desirée did too. They held on to the pole and their sneakers quickly went into second position, heels one foot apart. They zipped into third position.

"Fourth position," Marisol said, imitating Madame's tone. "Heel of right foot in front of the toes of the left foot." She threw open her arm for the port de bras and poked a man standing next to her.

"Oops, sorry," Marisol mumbled.

The man gave her an outraged look that made them giggle.

"We better skip fifth," Desirée whispered.

"Anyway, I'm gonna do every single thing Madame says."

"Me too." Desirée looked anxious. "You think a hot bath is important?"

"Well, she said, didn't she?"

"Oh."

"Sure sounds good to me," Marisol said. "What's the matter?"

Desirée shrugged.

"What?" Marisol asked again.

"There's no bathtub."

"Oh. Well . . . well, I bet a shower would be okay. Like a long hot steamy shower."

"I can't take a long shower; there's always someone waiting and yelling. There's only four stalls in the women's showers and no curtains, so I get out fast."

"You mean it's not private?"

"Nothing's private," Desirée said.

"Not even when you go to the bathroom?"

Desirée shook her head. "I can't look in the mirror in private, or even cry if I feel like it. There's always somebody. . . ."

Marisol's voice dropped. "Is it awful?"

"It's a family shelter, that's for people with kids, so

that makes it better. I was scared at night 'cause my bed was so far from my mother's, but last month I got a bed next to her and Dieudonné and Ti-Jean. So it's better now."

Marisol knew the shelter was the big gray building on Avenue A; that's all she knew about it. She'd never thought about the inside. "Desirée—don't families stay together in their own room?"

Desirée shook her head. "No, it's Tier One, with fathers, mothers, and kids all mixed up in one big place. We get a locker, that's all. But we might get moved up to a Tier Two shelter. If there's space. In Tier Two, that's where a family gets a room."

"That would be good," Marisol said.

"It would be good luck! Then my mother, she could take in sewing again."

"That would be good," Marisol repeated. She couldn't think of anything else to say.

She glanced over at Mrs. Joliecoeur. It had to be hard for her to keep herself and everybody so clean. Marisol looked down at Dieudonné hanging on to the pole next to her—he looked messy now, kind of sweaty, and his shirt had crept out of his pants and was hanging from under his jacket, but he'd started off neat and clean. And Desirée always looked scrubbed and starched; even the pink ribbons in her topknot looked starched. It had to be so extra hard.

Marisol thought about the way everybody in school

said the shelter kids stank. She and the Fab Four had said that too. It was true, some of them *did* smell bad, but she'd never given a thought to where they'd be washing up. The Joliecoeurs didn't smell at all, not one bit. Except for Ti-Jean; he started off sweet like baby powder, but by the end of the trip, he trailed an aura of spit-up and wet diapers—but all babies did, so that didn't count.

"You know what? You could come straight over to my house and use the tub. You can go first," Marisol said. "I don't have any of those—what-did-she-call-them—Epsom salts? I'll get my dad to buy some for next time."

"Thanks," Desirée said, "but I have to be there in time or I miss dinner. Thanks. It's okay if I ache tomorrow like she said."

They fell silent. They swayed with the motion of the train.

"Why does she call us little swans?" Desirée asked.

"I don't know." Marisol shrugged. "I guess that's better than turkeys."

Desirée's eyes got big. "Turkeys?"

"In American, that's a put-down. Oh, snap, what if 'swans' is a put-down in Russian?"

Desirée started to laugh. "'Cause swans don't turn out from the hip."

"No, no, no!" Marisol said, looking down her nose.

They were both laughing. Donny joined in, even

though he didn't know what it was all about, and that made them laugh harder.

96   She liked the Joliecoeurs, Marisol thought, and not just for getting her to ballet school. She really liked Desirée.

For the next class, Marisol clipped her hair back on both sides with some barrettes she'd found in her junk drawer. They were red plastic bows and they looked dorky. And even worse, she couldn't make them pull back her shaggy bangs or the short little wisps on the sides. She'd have to figure out something else, but there was no time; she had to meet the Joliecoeurs in a minute.

At least Madame didn't say anything about her hair in class.

Madame showed them a new stretch. They had to slide one leg up on the barre and bend their bodies over it sideways from the waist. Marisol couldn't bend her body anywhere near as low as Madame could, or even Desirée. She tried harder and it hurt.

At home that evening, she looked all around the apartment for something that was the right height. The kitchen table was higher than the barre, but it was the best thing around.

"Hey, get your foot off the table!" Luis yelled.

"Wait, I'm doing something."

"We gotta eat off that!"

"I'll wash it later. Anyway, my socks are clean."

Marisol got her leg up on the table okay, but when she tried the bend, her leg slid on the plastic top. There was nothing to hook her heel on. So she couldn't bend very far, but she felt that good ache in the back of her leg. . . .

"What're you doing?" Luis asked.

"Ballet."

"*That's* ballet?"

Marisol didn't answer. She was busy bending sideways, keeping her arm raised and round.

"No kidding," Luis said. "What're they teaching you?"

"You want to see?" Marisol held the table edge for support. "Look, these are the five positions."

"You need to go to school to move your feet around?"

"But look how good they're turned out. And this is ronds de jambe. That means circles with your legs. It's French."

"That don't look like any dancing," Luis said.

"It's *training*."

She had blurted it out just for something to say to Luis, but in bed that night, Marisol thought, that's exactly what it was! She was in training, like an Olympic athlete. With every single move, she was paring away the old Marisol body and turning herself into the strong, elastic dancer that she knew was underneath there somewhere.

Marisol sighed. Once a week was too slow—it would take forever.

She lay on her back. She straightened her legs under the blanket and turned out her feet. *From the hip*, she could hear Madame reminding her. If she could keep them that way all night, every night, her turnout would get perfect so fast.

"Luis?"

No answer from the bed across the room.

"Luis?" A little louder. "Are you sleeping?"

Luis groaned. "Not anymore." His words came out a yawn. "What's the matter?"

"I need you to tie my legs to the bed."

"What?"

"So they won't move when I'm asleep. Get my jump rope from the—"

"¡*Ay, bendito!* What else!"

"Come on, please—"

"It's bad enough I got to share a room with you—"

"It'll only take a minute—"

"Go tie your own legs if you want."

"Come on, I can't by myself. Come on, Luis—"

"Tie up your mouth, too, while you're at it. Let me sleep or I'm gonna move your bed out to the kitchen."

It wasn't a big thing to ask, Marisol thought. She'd do lots more for him. Well, he'd have to untie her legs in the morning, but that wouldn't take him long. She'd better not ask again, though, because he sounded too mad.

He hated having to share a room with her, that was the truth. She liked it. She liked hearing him breathe and she'd feel lonely without him there. But Luis wouldn't be lonely for her at all. He'd probably be happy if she disappeared for good.

Somehow she'd keep her legs in position without his help. She willed herself not to move in her sleep. But she woke up in the morning all curled up on her side, with her knees tucked against her chest.

Marisol tried to concentrate on her turnout in school, too. But then Gloria said, "How come you're walking like a duck?"

"Because I feel like it," Marisol mumbled.

Gloria gave her a funny look. "Well, don't. It looks weird."

So she went back to walking the regular way.

It would be so great if Gloria was in ballet too, Marisol thought.

Gloria had been her best friend forever, from the time they shared the clay on the second day of kindergarten. And it wasn't only that. Papi was friends with Gloria's parents; they went to Iglesia de Cristo too. She and Gloria had their first communion together and their beautiful white dresses were almost the same, except that Gloria's had more lace on top. They were just like sisters. And then they became friends with Katie in second grade, and when Linda moved to the neighborhood, she fit right in. The Fab Four thought alike and acted alike.

In class, they slouched in their seats the same way, a cool kind of slouch like they didn't care too much about anything.

But Madame's words were echoing in Marisol's head. "Lift up your ribs so your chest feels high. Chin up." So Marisol sat up tall and proud, the *dancer's* way. The funny thing was that sitting up made her feel more alert; it was easier to pay attention to Mrs. Lonigan.

She looked around the room. The rest of the Fab Four was in the usual pose. And there was Desirée, sitting with her back extra straight and her head high. Their eyes met; they both lifted their ribs another fraction and smiled at each other. Desirée knew.

Marisol didn't get to see her Big Sister until the Sunday after the third ballet class, because Jeanne's rotation had her working some weekends.

It was getting cold, but it was a sunny day.

"It'll be real winter soon," Jeanne said. "It feels like the last chance to do something outdoors."

Jeanne took her uptown, to Central Park. They went through the zoo. They watched some men sailing boats in the Boat Basin. Then they stopped to get hot dogs from a vendor. Jeanne was nice; she always treated.

Marisol swallowed a big bite and then continued with what she'd been telling Jeanne. ". . . and the problem is"—she licked stray mustard from her lips—"there's nothing to show anybody. I did a pas de bourrée for my friend Gloria—we learned that last time; it's hard to do right and I'm the *best* at it—but she didn't think it was so special. She was nice and everything, but I could tell. I guess it doesn't look like much."

"What's a pas de . . ." Jeanne smiled. "Whatever you said."

"You change weight *three* times. You start in a demi-plié with one foot behind, and then you jump and change feet. You never have two feet on the ground at the same time."

"It certainly sounds hard," Jeanne said.

"*And* you have to land light. But we're not learning anything flashy, not yet."

"The important thing is you're having fun," Jeanne said.

"It's not fun, exactly." Marisol took the last bite and wiped her lips with the napkin. "Everything's *discipline*. You have to keep quiet and concentrate all the time."

"I know that," Jeanne said. "I meant that you like it."

"I do. So does my friend Desirée. But two girls in the class dropped out already."

They followed a winding path. There were bushes with scarlet leaves. Fallen leaves crunched under their feet. Most of the tree branches were already bare. It still smelled green, like far away in the country. But over and above the trees, Marisol could see the towers of sky-scrapers in the distance. She liked the reminder that she was still in her city.

"There's an old movie you have to see, Marisol. *The Red Shoes*," Jeanne said. "It's probably on video, but you should see it on a big screen. Every once in a while it comes around again; I'll watch the papers and I'll definitely take you."

"Who's in it?"

"Moira Shearer."

"I never heard of her."

"I told you, it's an old movie. It's *the* great ballet film. Every girl who saw it wanted to become a ballerina on the spot."

"You too?"

"Sure, for about five minutes." Jeanne laughed. "I'm a good athlete, but I'm no dancer. Always had two left feet when it came to dancing."

"What's the movie about?"

"Remember the fairy tale about the girl who puts on red shoes and they make her dance and dance and dance? At first it's wonderful, but then she can't stop."

"What happens?"

"She has to keep on dancing, until she's exhausted."

It sounded vaguely familiar to Marisol. "She dies, right?"

"Well, yes."

"That's not such a nice fairy tale."

"The movie's based on it, but it's different. The ballerina has to keep on dancing because that's where her heart is. She even gives up her true love and—"

"She shouldn't have to give up *love!*"

"Being a ballerina takes all her time and energy. She wants to be great."

"She still shouldn't give up love. Does she die at the end too?"

"Yes, because she's very sick and she's not supposed to exert herself at all, but she can't give up dancing. A famous choreographer makes a ballet especially for her and dancing it is the triumph of her life. So she dies gloriously, for her art."

"It would be better if she danced gloriously and stayed healthy," Marisol said.

"I think I told it wrong," Jeanne said. "I don't remember it all that well, except that it was beautiful and romantic. I know you'd love it."

Marisol was too polite to disagree. But it was okay with her if that movie *never* came around.

The barrettes didn't work. For the next three Wednesdays, Marisol tied a ribbon in her hair. She was letting her bangs grow in and they were almost over her eyes now; the ribbon held them back pretty well. It caught some of the little side wisps, too. But the ribbon would start slipping during class. It bothered her; she had to keep retying it.

If she had a magic lantern for only one wish, she thought, she'd wish for a dancer's bun on top of her head. Why did hair have to grow so *slow*?

One evening, she suddenly thought of the perfect thing: a sweatband! Luis had a blue one that he wore for soccer. How come she didn't think of that before? It would hold everything back, and look professional, too.

She knew exactly where Luis kept it—the middle dresser drawer with his socks and T-shirts. She was itching to try it on. It would be easy to find, and she was awfully tempted, but Luis was a nutcase about *privacy*. One time she'd gone into his drawer without asking first and he was furious. "Hands off my stuff!" he'd yelled right in her face. "Can't I have one single thing here that's private?" He went on and on, and made her cry.

And if she borrowed something without asking, even if it was out on *top* of the dresser, even if it was a little thing that she knew he'd give her anyway, he got so mad he'd throw things around. With Luis, you had to get written permission.

So Marisol waited. Luis should have been home already; maybe they were doing a big cleanup at the Isla Verde. Five minutes. She wasn't good at being patient. She had her hand on the knob of his drawer—but then she thought maybe she'd better run downstairs and ask him. It wasn't that late, even if it was dark out—it seemed to be getting dark earlier every day—and she'd be home again in a minute. She didn't feel like putting her sneakers on again, but that was better than having Luis yell at her.

Avenue C looked like midnight. The streetlamp emphasized the shadows in pockmarked, peeling bricks. Some raggedy men were warming up around a fire in a trash can. Marisol walked by fast. The Isla Verde was only another half block. . . .

But the Isla Verde was closed. Heavy steel shutters were down over the windows and door. The bright colors of Chico's mural looked dim in the half-light.

It was okay, she told herself, the real night people wouldn't be out yet. But maybe Papi had good reasons for wanting her home before dark. She zipped up her jacket against the cold.

She looked around in confusion. Where *was* Luis?

The only place on the block with its lights on was the little bodega on the corner. She could hear salsa blasting from the doorway. There was a gang of boys in front. She came closer. She recognized the maroon jacket with black stripes—Eddie, Luis's friend. Luis would be there too. She ran the rest of the way—but Luis wasn't with the group outside.

"Where's my brother?" she asked, out of breath.

"Hey, Marisol," Eddie said. He turned toward the doorway. "Yo, anybody know where Perez went?"

"He's at Los Hermanos," a voice from inside called.

"Your father know you're out?" Eddie asked. "You got a problem?"

"No, it's okay." Marisol took a breath. "Thanks."

She headed toward Los Hermanos. Three blocks. There was a man, weaving and mumbling, approaching her on the sidewalk. He had a bandanna tied around long, stringy gray hair. His bony chest was naked. She could outrun him if she had to, she thought. But he passed right by her, in another world, muttering words that made no sense. His eyes looked blind.

The streetlamp on Fourth was broken. The entrances to the alleys she passed were pitch-black. Marisol shivered.

Somewhere a woman was yelling, and then Marisol heard the crash of a bottle.

The lights outside Los Hermanos blinked on and off,

red and yellow. She saw the big German shepherd tied to a lamppost. Tito's guard dog. He was waiting, patient and quiet, but she made a careful circle around him on her way to the glass door. The smells of liquor, sofrito, and chicken mingled in the cold air. She peeked in. The place was mostly empty. One table had a group of men crowded around it. One of them was laughing, his mouth wide open, white teeth glinting in the light. And then she saw Luis sitting with them.

Marisol backed away from the door. She stood stock-still for a moment. She couldn't move. Then she started running for home.

There was a friendly face—Mr. Rodriguez, coming home from work, still wearing hospital white. But she barely returned his greeting. Running, running. And then a teenage girl—Norma Jimeniz, swinging down the side-walk, skinny and pale as a ghost, skinny legs under a shiny skirt that barely covered her. Marisol could remember back when Norma helped her dress Barbie dolls. Everyone knew that Norma had become a puta for crack. Their eyes met, but they didn't say anything.

Marisol wanted to cry—for Norma, for Luis, for Papi, for everybody, even for the patient dog.

She ought to tell Papi, Marisol thought.

If she told, Luis would never trust her again.

Maybe there was nothing to tell. Maybe Luis had delivered something from Isla Verde or the bodega, and

Tito treated him to chicken, like the last time, and that was all. Maybe it was only the second time. But in the glimpse she'd caught of Luis, he looked too comfortable.

She couldn't say anything to Luis; he'd think she'd been spying on him.

¡Ay, Santo Dios! How could she tell Papi? It would break his heart. And he'd still have to go to work every day. He couldn't stay home to hold Luis's hand.

She heard the key in the lock and then Luis was in the kitchen in front of her, wriggling out of his jacket, looking as normal as every day, looking like her brother.

"Eddie said you wanted me?" he said.

"Oh. Yeah."

"What's up?"

Marisol shrugged.

"How come you went out?"

"I only went to the Isla Verde. I was looking for you. It was closed."

"Uh-huh."

"Where were you?" she asked.

"Just hanging."

"You're still working at the Isle Verde?"

"Sure, why?"

"Because it was closed."

"We close at six except Fridays. Papi home yet?"

"No."

"So why were you looking for me?"

"Oh. That." It seemed like ages and ages ago, before

she had to carry this burden.

Luis was looking at her, waiting.

She bit her lip. "I want to wear your sweatband Wednesday. I wanted to try it on."

"Okay, I'll go get it."

If she asked first, he was always generous. He was great that way.

She followed him into their room.

He took it out of the drawer and tossed it. "Here."

"Thanks." She left the band dangling from her fingers. She watched him closely.

"What do you need it for?"

"For ballet."

"You don't raise no sweat in 'ballet.'" He said the word in falsetto.

And Marisol was suddenly so angry, she wanted to punch the smile off his face! "You don't know nothing about it! It's *all* sweat!"

"Whoa. What're you mad for?"

"You think you're so smart! It's tougher than soccer!"

"Okay. All right."

"I'm doing something *good*. I'm not doing anything stupid." Her voice cracked. She was on the edge of tears.

"I didn't know you took it that serious."

"I do." She turned from him. "It's my dream."

"Okay," he said.

She sagged down on the edge of her bed. "You need to have one too, Luis."

"I got a million of them."

"What?"

"The bike, Air Jordans, in-line skates, a dynamite car, a big apartment with my own room, airplane tickets to go anyplace I—"

"A dream isn't about things," Marisol said. "A dream is who you want to be. Who you want to become."

Luis shrugged. Marisol twisted the sweatband around and around on her wrist.

The scream of an ambulance siren blasted through the room. It had to be awful to be rushing to the hospital in the night, Marisol thought, with someone you love lying there and maybe dying.

The siren slowly faded off into the distance.

"It's not tougher than soccer, though," Luis said.

"Dancers have to make it look easy; they're not allowed to grunt and groan." Ballet was something Marisol could talk about. Otherwise, she couldn't think of a thing to say to him.

"They're tougher athletes than anybody," Marisol continued. "It's like body-building, like Arnold Schwarzenegger, only different muscles."

Luis raised his eyebrows with that look he had.

"Okay," Marisol said, "see if you can do this."

She pushed a chair out of the way and lay down on the floor, flat on her stomach. Then she raised one leg as high as she could behind her—and it was high. She was getting lots better.

Luis flopped down next to her.

"You can't move your body," she told him. He got his leg up pretty well—he was a natural athlete.

"You gotta keep it straight and point your toe." Marisol took a breath and gathered together her very best effort. "See if you can get it as high as this," she said, "and hold it."

He strained for height, but he couldn't come close. "Jeez," he breathed. "That kills my back."

"Now try doing that ten times and then the other leg."

"No, thanks." He laughed and sat up cross-legged on the floor.

Marisol sat up too, her knees almost touching his. Both of them on the floor, she thought, side by side, like when they were little kids and playing, with nothing to fear.

"You're good," he said.

"Because I practice it every day," she said. "That's preparation for the arabesque."

He studied her face. "You're gonna be terrific, Marisol." He nodded and smiled. "You're gonna blow everyone away."

Finally, finally, he was showing respect, giving her dignidad. It was good to feel tight with him again. She wished it didn't have to make her feel so sad.

Marisol sat next to Gloria at the big table in the after-school program and watched her start another pot holder. Gloria had made more pot holders by now than anybody could have pots! Marisol admired how quickly she got it started, neatly looping the yarn over the needle.

Gloria glanced up. "I'll start yours if you want me to."

"I don't want another one. What do you need them for, anyway?"

"I don't know. I like the colors. See, I'm starting this one red and then I'm gonna put a yellow triangle in the middle. You think that'll look good? Red and yellow?"

"I guess."

Marisol looked around the room restlessly. There was the table of knitters, and the homework table where some of the kids were working. Luz Ortiz and Keisha Scott were sharing crayons and drawing on the same paper. Marisol couldn't figure out how they managed to draw together; she always had to do a picture her own way.

There was nothing she wanted to do. The after-school

program was better in warm weather when they got to play outside.

But then Marisol had a terrific idea, just as Mrs. Hollings, the knitting lady, was walking by.

"Mrs. Hollings! Can I make leg warmers?"

"Leg warmers?"

"Those knit things that go over your jeans to keep your legs warm."

"I know what they are, Marisol. I'd have to find a pattern." Mrs. Hollings looked at her doubtfully. "That's a big project; it would take quite a lot of wool."

"Oh." The truth was, Marisol was a rotten knitter. Her stitches were uneven and she kept dropping them, too. Her one and only pot holder was a mess. Papi was nice to hang it up in the kitchen, but it was an eyesore.

"I suppose if you brought in some yarn . . ." Mrs. Hollings was saying. "Are you sure you want . . ."

"Never mind, I guess not," Marisol said. It would be a miracle if she finished one, much less two.

"Teach! Help me!" someone called, and Mrs. Hollings wandered away.

Gloria finished the beginning row with a sigh of satisfaction. "What do you want leg warmers for? Nobody wears them."

"Yes, they do," Marisol said. "Almost all the dancers I see in the elevator. It's important to keep your muscles warm. Last time, when we walked to the train after class, my legs got cold; the wind went right through my jeans."

Gloria looked blank.

"And it's only November," Marisol continued. "I wish I had a long, long coat!"

"You'd look weird." Gloria wound the yarn around and pushed the needle through. "Everybody wears parkas."

"I don't care. See, if your leg muscles get chilled right after ballet, that makes them stiff."

Gloria was silent for a minute. Then she looked at Marisol. "No offense, but I'm gonna tell you something."

Anything that started with "no offense" made Marisol nervous. "What?"

"You keep talking about your ballet. That's all you ever talk about."

"No, it's not."

"Linda and Katie were saying that too."

"Linda and Katie said that?"

"It's not like I don't understand, kind of. I mean, remember last year, when I first got Violet? I was all excited about having a new little kitten, I never had a pet before, so I was always talking about the cute things she did and stuff. Remember? But then I stopped. But you been going on for months with ballet, ballet. So I'm telling you, for your own good."

"Thanks a lot," Marisol said stiffly.

"You don't have to get mad."

"Well, I don't care about pot holders and you're talking yellow triangles! And you guys are in love with

Michael Jackson and I think he moves like a windup toy, so what? I listen to you anyway. I think he's squirrely and"—Marisol rolled her eyes—"and I'm not gonna be in love with Michael Jackson! But I don't say anything."

Gloria's tone turned sharp. "You don't have to think you're better than everybody just because—"

"I don't think I'm better," Marisol said softly, through the hurt.

"—just because you got picked. You changed a whole lot, Marisol."

"No, I didn't," she said.

Gloria frowned at her knitting. Marisol watched the silver needles flash in the light.

She *wanted* to be one of the Fab Four, comfortable like always, acting and thinking alike. Papi always said, "Be true to yourself," but what he meant was not doing something stupid like drugs just because your friends did. But the Fab Four weren't into anything bad. Gloria, Linda, and Katie were regular people from the neighborhood, good straight people like Papi and—and Luis.

She didn't truly fit in with the uptown girls in ballet class. Claire was very friendly, but Marisol knew without even asking that her mother would never let her come to play on Avenue C.

"You're always with that shelter kid," Gloria said.

"Desirée's okay," Marisol said. "She's nice."

"She's too quiet," Gloria said. "She's so shy."

Marisol nodded. She couldn't argue with that.

There was a lot about Desirée's life and family that was strange to her. She liked her, but Desirée wasn't an almost-sister like Gloria.

The uptown girls, and Madame too, talked different. It was still English, but different from the neighborhood—straight out of Mrs. Lonigan's grammar book. No double negatives. "You've been" instead of Gloria's "You been going on for months. . . ." Their words came out crisper. And once in a while, Marisol had deliberately imitated them. Was she sounding snotty? Did that mean she wasn't being true to herself and everybody she loved?

She didn't call out in class anymore and she had started doing all the homework because she was practicing *discipline*. Even Mrs. Lonigan had noticed. But she wasn't really changing, was she? Just because she was doing a few things different—differently.

Gloria's needles clicked.

The overhead light buzzed.

"I could stop taking ballet anytime I want to," Marisol said. No red shoes on *her* feet!

Gloria looked up at her.

"But not yet," Marisol added quickly.

Marisol had to tell someone. Not Gloria, because she knew Marisol's family too well. Desirée didn't know Luis at all. And it was easier to trade secrets in the subway on the way to ballet, with the train's roar filling in all the silences.

"My brother looks up to that man Tito," Marisol said. "I think he might be getting in trouble."

Desirée listened quietly.

"See, Tito dresses sharp, he looks *good*. He lights his cigarettes with dollar bills; that's the truth, people have seen him. Maybe he's more of a big shot than Papi, but—" Marisol cleared her throat. "I can understand someone wanting to be like him, but—"

The train lurched to a stop at Thirty-fourth Street. More people got on. The doors whooshed shut and the train started again.

"I wish no one invented drugs or guns," Marisol said.

"I wish my mother spoke English," Desirée whispered. "She's embarrassed to make mistakes, so she won't try."

They swayed with the motion as the train picked up speed.

Desirée kept her eyes on the floor. "When I speak for her, people treat *me* like the grown-up. It makes me feel bad."

"I'm scared for Luis," Marisol said. "At night, I have bad visions."

Desirée's voice dropped even lower. "I'm ashamed of being ashamed."

There were so many people who had things weighing them down, Marisol thought. Even the uptown girls.

Jennifer, the one with the long brown curls, got dressed extra quick in the dressing room one day, but

Marisol caught a flash of bruises all over her legs. And someone whispered that Jennifer's father got out of control when he drank.

Claire told Marisol that Tracy's family was superrich and knew *everybody*, but Tracy's big sister was seriously retarded—she was sixteen and she couldn't walk yet. All their money and pull couldn't fix her.

It didn't ease your own pain just because you had lots of company, Marisol decided. All you could do was keep your back straight and your head high.

It was the last ballet class before Christmas vacation and Marisol was so excited that she could hardly keep count with the piano. Inside her, everything was going double-time. Because after class, they were going to see a real live ballet!

Madame had made the announcement last week. "The company's dress rehearsal of *Swan Lake* is next Wednesday. Marguerite DeFries is dancing Odette/Odile. If you wish to stay after class, you have an opportunity to see the first act. Be sure to tell anyone picking you up to come an hour later."

Mrs. Joliecoeur said no at first; more than two hours of waiting with the baby and Dieudonné! Marisol prodded Desirée to beg and plead, and Mrs. Joliecoeur finally gave in.

They did the usual barre exercises and center work. Madame didn't say a word about *Swan Lake* and Marisol worried that she had forgotten all about it. But after the reverence, instead of going to the dressing room, they gathered in the hall. The only one who didn't stay was Tracy; her family was flying to Palm Beach that night.

Madame herded them down the hall and into the elevator. Desirée looked worriedly at her mother and brothers as she passed the waiting room. Marisol could hear the baby's whimper and Mrs. Joliecoeur's soft singsong.

They went all the way down to the basement. There was a long passageway, at least as long as a city block, with twists and turns and corridors and signs saying PARKING. Marisol thought she could get lost there in a minute and made sure to keep up with the group.

"Remember, you must be absolutely still. As quiet as little mice," Madame told them.

Marisol almost giggled. Mostly they were "little swans," now they were "little mice." What next?

They went into another elevator, and Marisol blinked when the door opened. They came out into a huge lobby with bright crystal lights and double staircases covered with red velvet!

"On tiptoe, no noise," Madame said as she led them into the auditorium.

Rows and rows of empty seats in the dark. Madame led them down the long center aisle to the second row. The first row was filled with red leotards, the third-year class. Marisol looked at them with admiration and envy.

"*Vite, vite,* quickly."

They filed into their seats. A heavy velvet curtain covered the stage. Marisol waited. Nothing was happening. She craned her neck to look around. There were balconies— three rows of balconies! And boxes high on the sides!

"There's Peter Jovine," Claire whispered to Marisol. There were three men sitting in a middle row.

"Which one?" Marisol whispered back. She'd heard his name often. Peter Jovine was the head choreographer and the boss of everything at Manhattan Ballet. If he liked someone, then they could be in the company.

"With the long white scarf," Claire said.

Marisol turned and stared at him.

On Marisol's other side, Desirée whispered, "I hope my mother's okay."

"Shhh," Madame said from behind them.

They waited.

No movie theater was anything like this, Marisol thought.

From somewhere came the discordant sounds of instruments tuning up. There was a buzz of anticipation. Marisol sat forward, watching for the curtain to move.

What happened next surprised her. A spotlight went on and a whole orchestra came into view, rising up on a platform in front of the curtain.

Music swelled up. Marisol's ears and heart filled with sound. The melody had sadness in it, and wonder, and magic. It made her ache for—something. And it made her happy too, all at the same time.

The curtain slowly rose on white and silvery trees and pale-blue moonlight. The dancers came out in a long row, in filmy white costumes, fluidly gliding into the melody. They formed into a circle of long white necks swooping low. In the center, Odette's feathered headdress glittered silver and white under the lights. She floated across the stage. When the man carrying a bow and arrow came forward, her hands went up in shivering fear. Marisol felt her fear, every bit of it. And Odette made turns—on one toe!—as fast and electric as lightning. The man hovered in the air at the top of his leap, suspended in time—it was impossible, no one could do that! And the pas de deux—they were declaring their love in thrilling movement, more true and passionate than words. And the music. And then Odette, limp with sorrow, dancing as though the bones in her body had melted from sadness. And the row of beating arms, swan wings ready to ride away on a passing breeze.

Marisol was in a trance. She didn't know her mouth was open. She barely breathed.

The curtain fell. "First intermission," someone whispered.

"Come, ladies," Madame said.

"Can't we stay?" someone pleaded.

"No, your nannies are waiting," Madame said, "and I have my next class."

Marisol gripped the arms of her seat. It wasn't until Claire nudged her that she could rise and file out with everyone else.

In the elevator, in the passageway, in the other elevator, the vision of silver and white and blue stayed behind her eyes.

And the melody at the beginning. She couldn't lose that melody.

Desirée tugged at her in front of the dressing room. "Let's hurry, my mother's—"

"In a minute," Marisol said.

Madame was in the doorway of the studio. Marisol had to know. She walked toward her. Madame intimidated her, but she *had* to . . .

"Madame?" she said.

"Yes?" The eagle eyes looked down at her.

"The music. What was that music?"

Madame raised an eyebrow. "*Swan Lake.*"

"Yes, but who's it by?"

"Tchaikovsky."

"Okay. Thanks." She started to go.

"Wait—did you like it?"

"It was wonderful!"

"You know, I chose you because I thought I saw musicality." Madame's smile made lines in the makeup around her eyes. "I think I made a good choice, Marisol."

"Oh!" Marisol didn't know that Madame even knew her name! "Thank you!" She wanted to do a reverence, but instead backed off, flustered. "And thank you for *Swan Lake!*"

In the dressing room she changed automatically, lost in a dream. *Tchai-kovsky,* she repeated to herself, *Tchai-kovsky.* She followed Desirée out of the building, hugging Madame's words to herself all the way.

"That's what ballet is," Marisol said to Desirée. "It's not just amazing steps. It's acting too, and feeling!" She couldn't find the right words to describe this revelation and her sharp joy. "I loved it so much," she finally said.

"Me too," Desirée said.

Marisol wanted to fly over the street, spread her swan wings and soar over the honking taxis. "I'm gonna practice extra, every day, all the time. I've got to dance Odette! Remember the part where she—"

"I wouldn't want to be on a big stage like that, in front of everybody," Desirée said. "Strangers and everybody watching. I bet there were hundreds of seats."

Marisol looked at Desirée in surprise. "We've got to go on stage. . . ."

"You heard what Claire said before. Marguerite DeFries's toes bleed after every performance. Her feet are all knobby, gnarly and ugly."

"Claire didn't see them."

"Yeah, but her sister did."

"But you still want to be a dancer, don't you?"

"I don't know," Desirée said.

What was the matter with her? Madame had chosen her too, Marisol thought. Desirée had a natural body for it. How could she not want—

"And by the time you're thirty, you're too old," Desirée said, "and you have to go looking for another job anyway."

"I thought you liked it," Marisol said.

"I do," Desirée said. "I don't think I want it the way you do."

"Then—what do you like so much about ballet?"

"I like being in class. I like the way it's peaceful and you always know what to expect. It makes me feel safe."

Safe? It made Marisol feel anything but safe. It was scary to want something—*need* something—so much. She knew she was hooked, forever and ever.

Their Christmas was half Puerto Rican, half New York style; Nuyorican, just like Marisol and Luis, Papi said.

It started three days ahead, when Papi prepared the marinade for the roast pork. Marisol perched on a stool, with her feet wrapped around the rungs, and watched him chop the onions on the kitchen counter.

"I got some nice loin," Papi said. He pushed the cut-up onions into a hill with the blade of the knife and chopped them smaller and smaller. "Now, at home, we'd roast a whole pig outdoors for Christmas. I helped dig the pit."

Marisol knew "at home" meant in the countryside outside Bayamón.

"My papi and tío Horacio tied the pig by its legs and Papi cut the neck with one quick stroke. A necklace of blood, and my mami caught the blood and guts in her big blue bowl."

"Yuk," Marisol said.

"No yuks! The smell of those sausages frying . . ." Papi scraped the onions into the giant pan into which he had poured a jug of red wine. He minced the garlic. "Then my mami, tía Delsa, and tía Leona ground a mountain of plantains, *yautía*, and *yuca* for the *pasteles* until their knuckles were raw."

He was chopping a bunch of cilantro. Marisol picked up a leafy sprig and chewed on it.

"Maybe next year, I'll take you to Puerto Rico to visit your *abuela*. I got a week coming to me."

"Let's go!" Papi always made the way he grew up sound so nice—summertime all year long, always barefoot in the grass, sleeping in hammocks, playing around free with no dangers except for fire ants.

"I'll see," he said. "Get the rosemary."

Marisol hopped down and handed him the little bottle from the cabinet.

"Did my mother make *pasteles* too?"

"No, not my Maria." Papi smiled. "She was a city girl from Santurce. She had beautiful hands."

"Her face was beautiful too, right?" Marisol asked. "Like in the photo?"

"The first time I saw her, at her uncle's house, I stared and stared," Papi said. "Fifteen and a beauty. She knew I was looking, but she kept her eyes down, like a lady. But there was a little smile she couldn't hold back, so I knew she liked me. Now the pepper."

Marisol shook the pepper mill so the black peppercorns at the bottom wouldn't jam up.

"Give it five good twists," Papi said.

The sharp aroma hit her nose.

"Do I take after her?" Marisol asked hopefully.

"No, mi *tesoro*, you're from my side." He dipped his finger in the marinade and put a dab on the tip of Marisol's nose.

She brushed it off, unsmiling. She shouldn't have asked that stupid question, she thought. Her hands were rough and chapped all winter. And if someone stared at her, she'd stare right back. Papi had told her more than once to show respect for grown-ups by lowering her eyes, but she forgot and anyway, she didn't want to—she was one hundred percent Americana that way. No one would call her ladylike. Papi had to be disappointed.

Papi stirred the liquid. "Okay, I'm done."

"When are we getting the tree?" Marisol said.

"Later. When the prices go down."

In Puerto Rico, Papi didn't have a Christmas tree; they'd string lights and crepe-paper flowers over the bushes outside his house. Here, they strung lights all over the fire escape.

Papi put the pork into the pan; it pushed the marinade way up the sides, almost to overflowing.

"Don't forget, turn the meat every day," Papi said. "Tell Luis to help you lift it."

"Okay." Marisol shoved a container of milk out of the way as Papi carefully slid the pan onto the refrigerator shelf.

"And we'd put hay for the camels of the three magi out in the yard . . ." he said.

Marisol smiled, remembering. When she and Luis were little, they couldn't find hay *anywhere* on Avenue C. Luis decided camels would like Corn Flakes, too, and he was right, because the magi never disappointed them. They always found cellophane-wrapped candies in their shoes on Christmas morning.

Three more days to go!

It snowed on Sunday. Marisol and Luis slogged through the slush on Broadway and Fourth. They'd decided Tower Records was the place to get Papi's presents. The store was crowded and overheated; it smelled of wet wool. There were bins and bins of tapes and CDs. Luis led the way to the Latin section.

Luis flipped through tapes. "Carlos Montoya." Luis studied the cover. "There's boleros on this."

"That's good. He likes boleros," Marisol said.

"What else? We have to get two."

"How about this Rey Ruiz?" Marisol said.

"I was thinking guitarists for Papi."

"Ruiz is a terrific singer. Papi can dance to his songs."

"Maybe," Luis said. "I'll get him Montoya and you get him Ruiz?"

"I'm not sure. . . . You look some more; I'll be right back." She started down the aisle. "I want to see something."

"Meet me right back here," Luis said. "Don't get lost."

"Right! Like I'd get lost in Tower Records!"

She made a wrong turn before she found the classical music. She looked all through the C's. Nothing. Finally, she saw a salesman. Oh, snap, he was busy with a grown-up couple. She had to wait so long and she only had one little question.

They stopped talking for a moment, so she had a chance to say, "Mister, do you have Tchai-kovsky?"

"Yes." He turned away as if she were a black fly pestering him.

"Where? I looked in all the C's!"

"Try under T." There was a smirk on his face.

"T?"

"Tchaikovsky. With a T. T-C-H-A-I . . ."

"Oh." It *sounded* like it should start with C-H—she was a good speller! The grown-up couple seemed about to laugh. How was she supposed to know? She whirled away, furious and embarrassed.

She was suddenly conscious of the rip in the nylon shell of her parka that enlarged the pocket and showed the material underneath.

In the T's, so many tapes and all by Tchaikovsky! This guy was sure keeping busy. *Nutcracker Suite, 1812 Overture, Piano Concerto* . . . She wanted to hear everything he wrote. And then—*Swan Lake.* The cover had a dreamy, fuzzy photo of a ballerina.

She elbowed her way back to Luis.

"I found Manitas de Plata! He's that Gypsy dude in Spain plays flamenco," Luis said. "Papi loves that."

"Wait," she said. "Papi might like this." She held up *Swan Lake*.

Luis took it from her. He studied the picture. "What is it?"

"You should hear it, it's so—"

"Ballet music? You want to get Papi *ballet* music?"

"He'd like it," she said stubbornly.

"Good going, Marisol. You get him ballet music and I'll get him a catcher's mitt that just so happens to fit my hand."

Under Luis's scornful look, she reluctantly went to return *Swan Lake*.

Maybe they'd have it at the library. One way or another, she had to hear that music again.

In Puerto Rico, Marisol knew, Christmas meant *parrandas*: all the people going from house to house, eating, dancing, and singing *aguinaldos*, the Christmas songs.

The sidewalk of Avenue C in front of the apartment buildings was no place for *parrandas*. Instead, they had lots of people come over on Christmas Eve.

Tía Mercedes, Papi's sister and Marisol's favorite aunt, came from the Bronx with her husband and the three little kids. They brought *tembleque*; Marisol loved anything with coconut!

Tía Alicia, Tío Hector, and her older cousin Julio came.

And Papi's good friend Raymond. His mustache tickled. "*¡Ay, qué linda!*" he said, and Marisol self-consciously smoothed her good red dress.

And the Marins from the apartment right below. Mrs. Marin was much too fat and trailed fumes of face powder. Marisol saw Luis wince when she came close and pinched his cheek.

And old Mrs. Garcia from across the street. She walked awfully slow now. It was okay that she'd been paid to watch her when she was little, Marisol thought. She *did* love Marisol; she could tell by the way Mrs. Garcia hugged and kissed her, held her at arm's length and said, "*Toda una señorita.*"

And Nina Matos, that bottle blonde who was always eyeing Papi, in a shiny dress cut so low that she could fall out any second! Papi must have invited her. Did he *like* her?

Though they'd moved all the furniture to the sides, the living room was soon overcrowded and some of the party crowded into the kitchen, too. The air was rich with aftershave, cologne, Tío Hector's cigar, roasted meat, and Barbancourt rum. Gold balls shone on their little tree in the corner. The lights on the fire escape twinkled in the dark outside. Other lights from across the street were reflected in their window.

When the salsa tapes went on, all the grown-ups danced, but after a while everyone moved back to make room and clapped to the beat as Papi swayed and twirled with Nina Matos. She was shaking her shoulders and working hard. He made everything look easy, his hips flowing as natural and sweet as syrup.

"Was my mother a good dancer too?" Marisol asked Tía Mercedes, squeezed next to her.

"Not like him," Mercedes said. "She was quiet. Gentle. And modest—she didn't like to be in the center." Mercedes laughed. "Antonio's a wild man! Look at him!"

Papi was going faster and faster, making up steps, doing make-believe flamenco, clapping his hands over his head. Nina couldn't keep up; she waved him away and backed off, laughing. Papi kept going by himself and everyone was clapping and yelling "Olé."

Luis's and Marisol's eyes met across the room; he was gonna love the Manitas de Plata.

Papi beckoned to her. "Come, m'hija!"

Marisol followed his steps and made up some of her own. They didn't know real flamenco and they didn't have taps on their shoes or castanets, but they kept their arms high over their heads and turned around each other in tighter and tighter circles and stamped out the rhythm triple-time. Good thing the Marins were right here at the party, Marisol thought, or they'd be banging on the pipes downstairs.

The music was hot and fast and bubbling in Marisol. Okay, she wasn't ladylike. Okay, she wasn't modest. The only person on earth who would call her toda una señorita— "all a young lady should be"—was old Mrs. Garcia. So what—she couldn't stop!

Papi was stamping against the floor as if he wanted to get free of the ground, free of anything holding him down, his back arched to lift himself up. Marisol thought, this was another way to fly!

After everyone left, Papi, Marisol, and Luis flopped down on the couch.

Papi looked around at the bits of food, napkins, half-filled glasses of rum-and-cola, and paper cups and plates strewn everywhere. He waved his arm over the mess and said, "Later."

"Okay, everyone's gone!" Marisol announced. "Now the presents!"

"Presents? For you?" Papi acted surprised. "Why? Have you two been polite and well-behaved all year?"

"Yes, Papi!" Marisol shouted. Luis rolled his eyes; he thought he was too cool for this.

"Remembered to wash behind your ears?"

"Yes, Papi." Marisol giggled.

They scattered to get boxes and bags from special hiding places.

Then there was a flurry of gift paper and ribbons. Papi said, "Montoya!" and "Manitas de Plata—hands of silver, for true!" It was a good choice; you could tell he was pleased. He smiled at Marisol. "But I'm danced out for tonight." She reached for his hand; she'd never felt closer to him.

Luis unwrapped the Swatch watch from Papi. "Hey, thanks! That's the exact design I wanted!" And he liked the black button-down shirt that Marisol had bought from a vendor on Sixth Street. It had the Polo logo on it, in red. The vendor said it was the real thing; even if it wasn't, it sure looked real. "Man, that's sharp! I wanna wear it right now. Thanks!"

Then it was Marisol's turn. Her present from Papi was in a big box. He leaned forward to watch her open it, his face full of pleasure, anticipating her excitement.

She fumbled with the stiff green wrapping paper. "What is it, what is it . . . "

She pried off the Scotch tape holding the lid.

She unfolded the tissue—something white, white net with sequins. . . . She lifted it out by the white satin top and fought to keep the dismay off her face. It was a tutu— a *costume*! "Thanks," she said. And then added, "It's pretty." She saw Luis giving her a hard look, indicating Papi with a tiny move of his chin. So she went to hug Papi.

"I think it's the right size," Papi said, "but you can exchange—"

"Oh, sure, it'll fit." She'd never wear it, never! How could he!

The puzzled expression on his face made her feel bad. She forced a big smile. "Oh, wow! Thank you, Papi!"

"Here." Luis handed her a Barnes & Noble shopping bag. "I didn't get it wrapped; there was a long line. . . ."

She was mystified. A book? She drew it out of the bag; it was big and heavy. *Prima Ballerina*. It was pages and pages, full-length photographs of famous ballerinas on one side and words all about them on the other. "Oh, Luis!" Anna Pavlova. Margot Fonteyn, in a breathtaking position. "Oh, Luis!"

He grinned. "You like it?"

"It's wonderful! How did you ever find . . . ?"

Later, in bed, she kept leafing through the book. Maria Tallchief—she looked Puerto Rican! No, she was American Indian. She danced in Firebird. Oh, she wanted to see a ballet called Firebird! Alicia Alonso—oh, snap, she was Cuban . . . but anyway, Latina. Natalia Makarova—she defected from Russia and—

Luis's voice interrupted her. "Listen, he tried. You should've said more to him. . . . It musta cost a lot. Jeez, I wish he'd asked me first. . . ."

"It's a play costume. He thinks I'm playing ballerina!"

"Yeah. Like if I got a fake Mets uniform 'cause I play ball."

"He doesn't respect—" she started.

"Don't hurt him. Tomorrow you put it on—"

"Right. For Halloween."

"—and show him and act thrilled."

"I know." She'd have to keep pretending. "Tomorrow."

"Okay," Luis said.

"But he doesn't understand the first thing about me!" It was almost insulting! "You knew; you got me the most perfect—"

"'Cause I see you. I see you work all the time. He

don't; he's not home. . . . You've grown up so quick."

Maybe that was true. Maybe last year she would have enjoyed a tutu costume.

Luis went to turn off the light.

"No, wait, leave it on a minute," she begged.

Marguerite DeFries was in the book! It said she'd trained at Manahattan Ballet School! . . . Suzanne Farrell . . . Maya Plisetskaya . . .

Marisol fell asleep with the light on, hugging *Prima Ballerina* to her chest.

On Monday, the first school day after Christmas vacation, Desirée rushed over to Marisol. "I have something to tell you."

"Me too," Marisol said. "I got the best book! I got to show you—"

"Marisol, stop talking," Mrs. Lonigan said. "In your seat now! You too, Desirée, sit down."

Desirée's seat was across the room. They didn't get a chance to talk again until reading; they sat together to be reading partners.

"I have good news," Desirée said. "Well, I guess good—and sort of bad. We found out yesterday."

"What?"

"We're moving up to Tier Two!"

"Tier Two," Marisol said. "Isn't that—"

"Marisol!" Mrs. Lonigan said. "Are you reading or talking?"

They looked down at the reader. Her ballet book was lots harder than this, with much bigger words, Marisol thought. She waited for Desirée to catch up before she turned the pages. At the end of the chapter there was a quiz; that's when they were allowed to talk to go over the answers.

"Isn't Tier Two where your family gets its own room?" Marisol asked.

Desirée nodded, excited.

"That's great! Your mom must be so happy." The Joliecoeurs deserved a break.

"There'll be a place to keep our things. I'll have my own drawer. And once we're in Tier Two, we might get moved up to Tier Three sometime and that's an *apartment!*"

"I'm so glad for you. That's wonderful news!"

"And it's in Brooklyn near my old school! I'll get to see my friends again."

"In Brooklyn?" Marisol stopped breathing.

"The bad part is, I'll miss you," Desirée said. "But we'll still see each other in ballet, right? My mother, she can take in sewing again, so she'll make the carfare. . . . It's lots farther to travel, but . . ."

Marisol couldn't answer. She couldn't even move.

Desirée looked worried. "You can get someone to take you, can't you?"

It took a while before Marisol could say, "I guess."

There was no one else!

"When?" Marisol said in a whisper.

"Tonight." It wasn't Desirée's fault that her eyes were shining.

Marisol thought and thought, all through math, all through social studies.

There was no one else. She'd gone through every possible person the first time around.

How could she get to ballet?

"The important thing to remember about the Civil War . . ." Mrs. Lonigan was saying.

How could she get to ballet?

Lunch. Gloria, Katie, and Linda chattered about their Christmas presents.

She could go by herself, Marisol thought, and not tell Papi.

Her sandwich tasted like cardboard.

That was a *huge* lie, one that she'd have to keep up all year. It would come between them, even if he didn't find out. And he would find out, sooner or later, and then he'd look at her differently. . . . She knew how Papi was. He wouldn't forget.

"So what did you get, Marisol?" Katie asked.

"What?"

"Your Christmas presents!"

"Oh. A—a dress from my dad and a book from Luis."

Walking home from East Houston in the dark by herself wouldn't be so great. Lying to Papi would be awful. How could she do that?

"Earth to Marisol!" Linda was saying. "What kind of dress?"

"Um—it's white with satin on top," Marisol said.

"Oooh, that sounds pretty."

Papi. Tía Mercedes. Jeanne Carlsen. Luis. Mrs. Garcia. She'd gone through them before. There was no one to take her.

It was even worse now. She'd already been to class. Now she'd know what she was missing.

"Marisol?" Gloria said. "Do you feel sick?"

Marisol shook her head.

"You don't look so good."

"I'm okay."

She was okay all through the afternoon. She was okay through the spelling quiz and through watching Mrs. Lonigan try to control Joey and through study time.

She told Gloria to go on to the after-school program without her.

Finally she was alone. She sat down on the front steps of the school and that's where the tears she'd been holding in all day exploded. She bent over her knees and buried her face in her arms. She cried with fierce, racking sobs that hurt her chest and filled her throat. She cried until there were no tears left. She banged her fist against the stairs. There was nothing she could do.

"Marisol!"

She looked up at Luis. She brushed her hand across her swollen, tear-stained cheeks.

"What happened? Somebody hurt you? Who? Where—?" He was tense and bristling, ready to fight.

She shook her head.

"What happened? Some kid came running into Isla Verde. 'Your sister's on the front steps bawling her eyes out.'"

Four teenage boys were dribbling a basketball along the sidewalk. Luis eyed them suspiciously.

"Who bothered you?" he demanded. "Which one?"

"Nobody." Marisol took a breath and got her voice under control. "Nothing like that. The people who used to take me to ballet—they're moving away. To Brooklyn."

Luis sat down next to her. "Oh."

"So I can't go anymore." She felt her face falling apart.

"Jeez, don't cry!"

"I'm not." She bit her lip hard.

He sat down next to her.

The thump of the basketball faded farther and farther away.

"That's not right," Luis said. "You ought to have a shot."

She felt the cold of the stone stairs through her jeans.

"I'm thinking," Luis said.

He took a tissue from his pocket and handed it to her. Marisol blew her nose and crushed the tissue into a tight wad in her fist.

It was cloudy. Everything on the street looked gray.

"I'll take you," he said.

"You will?"

Her heart must have shown in her face, because he said, "Hey, I ain't the Second Coming. I'm taking you to ballet, that's all."

"You'd do that for me? You'd have to wait there and—"

"No problem."

She smiled at him with shaky lips. "Thanks! Oh,
thanks!"

They sat for a while. "You okay now? I gotta get back
to work."

"Luis—what about Isla Verde?"

"I told you, no problem."

"But—"

"Trust me." Luis, as usual, kept his face stony, but
some kind of excitement was making his eyes glitter. "I
was thinking about quitting anyway."

There was a warning tingle down Marisol's back.
"Why?" she asked.

"Because it's a dumb job."

Marisol looked hard at him. "Are you working someplace else?"

"I can make a hundred times more in a New York
minute."

"Tito," she said.

"Can you keep your mouth shut?"

Marisol nodded.

"Swear?"

She nodded again, needing to know and afraid to
hear.

He shook his head. "No, forget it," he mumbled, but
some kind of excitement was popping out all over.

"Come on, what?" Marisol asked. "What?"

"He's smart, not just street smarts either. He's been

everyplace. Everything he does, man, it's class all the way. You should see him." The words poured out of him. "He likes me. He treats me like a man. He says I got brains, the way I can do long division in my head. He says brains count big with him."

"Are you working for him? *Are* you?"

"I didn't ask yet. But I been thinking."

"Yeah, brains count big with him," Marisol said. "Like Johnny Castro's."

"Castro's no good to him no more. He's a donkey. I wouldn't use. I'm not gonna waste that kind of cash up my nose. I figured I'd work for him a little while, not forever. Just long enough to—"

"It won't be for a little while."

"I don't want to talk no more." He stood up abruptly. "Ballet class day after tomorrow?"

"No, the new term starts next week."

"Okay, good, that's time to give Mr. Rivera notice. . . . I was going to anyway, sometime; doing it now works out perfect for you."

Marisol grabbed his arm. "Luis, don't! I'm scared! And what about Papi, he'd—"

He brushed her hand off roughly. "I said I'd take you. That's all you need to know."

"But—"

He shook his head disgustedly. "I shouldn't have said nothing."

She watched him go up the avenue, with his loose-hipped confident walk, until he got smaller and smaller and disappeared from sight.

At home, it was a strange evening. Luis wouldn't meet Marisol's eyes, though he glanced warily at her a couple of times. She could tell he was worried about blurting everything out. He got busy greasing his old skateboard on the kitchen table. He was rubbing the exact same spot over and over, shooting off nervous energy.

Marisol watched him in dumb misery.

Even Papi noticed. "How come it's so quiet around here?"

No one said anything.

Marisol went to the window. It was dark outside. Her reflection stared back at her: an ordinary kid with hunched shoulders. Automatically, she raised her ribs and straightened up. She'd learned to use the mirrors in the studio to check her position and mostly she saw herself straining and trying hard. But sometimes she thought she saw the dancer she could become. If she kept working at it. If she kept on going to class . . .

She wanted that more than anything, Marisol thought. Jeanne Carlsen said the lady in The Red Shoes even gave up love for dancing. After Swan Lake, she could kind of understand.

Luis said she ought to have a shot. She wanted it! Luis had offered her a way to keep on going. . . .

But she couldn't.

But she couldn't give up the dream of Odette either.

It would be fun to go uptown with Luis, better than feeling guilty because of Mrs. Joliecoeur and the crying baby.

But . . .

Marisol waited until after Papi was in the shower. She waited until she heard the water running before she spoke to Luis.

"Listen," she said, "forget about taking me to ballet. Not if it depends on you getting mixed up with Tito." It was the hardest thing she'd ever done; it left her feeling drained.

He looked up. "Did you think it was just for you?"

"No, but I don't want to be part of it."

"I would anyway, so you may as well get something from it."

She hesitated for a moment before she could say, "I don't want to get anything, not that way."

"What are you, the voice of my conscience?" Luis sounded mad. "I'm offering you a favor."

"Forget it," she said.

"Suit yourself."

So that was that, Marisol thought. She felt hollow.

Luis looked at her curiously. "I thought you were so hot for ballet."

"It means everything to me. "

"Then why?"

"Because you're my brother."

20

The uneasiness between Luis and Marisol lasted for days.

She *had* to tell Papi, Marisol thought, even though she'd sworn, even though Luis would hate her forever.

When Marisol passed Isla Verde in the afternoons, she always looked in to check. Luis was still there.

She was relieved; maybe she didn't have to tell yet. Thinking about it made her uncomfortable around Luis.

On Thursday evening they were waiting for Papi to come home for dinner. They were half watching *Hard Copy*. Normally they'd be talking all through it or jockeying for space on the couch, but now they were cautious around each other, distantly polite. The televison voices were the only ones in the room.

A blast of sirens and the screech of brakes came from outside; Luis turned the volume up.

Marisol could smell tomato sauce cooking next door—they always knew what the Viegas were having—and her stomach grumbled.

"Yeah, me too," Luis said. "What time is it?"

Marisol shrugged. "*Hard Copy* ends at seven thirty."

"Okay, if he 's not home by then, I'll make the burgers."

Later, that's how Marisol remembered exactly when it started. The show wasn't over yet; there was a commercial break.

At first Marisol heard a vague buzz of voices from outside, but her attention stayed on the supermodel's long, shining hair and she thought about trying Prell and maybe . . .

Suddenly everything seemed to hit at once—the buzz outside getting louder, the smell of acrid smoke, and a woman's wild screams, piercing as an arrow through the heart.

Smoke! It was her worst fear come true. "Fire! There's a fire!"

"Smells like rubber burning," Luis said.

She jumped up, her heart pounding. "The fire escape. The window guard!" What if the lock was rusty, what if . . . "Luis," she whimpered.

"You don't know it's us." He was moving too slow! He looked out the window. "Something's happening."

"Let's go! Luis! Let's get outta here!"

He headed for the door. She ran after him on shaky legs.

"Don't open it! If it's in the hall . . ." Everything they'd learned in Fire Prevention Week became jumbled in her mind. Get down low. Don't save anything.

"Cut it out, will ya? The door's cold."

He offered her his hand and she clutched it. They ran down the stairs.

Flames were shooting up in the middle of the street. Everything was confusion. Someone burning a tire. People milling together. A hoarse voice cursing. The sound of running feet pounding on the sidewalk. Cops standing around. The woman's inhuman screams, winding higher and higher. Voices harsh with anger.

"¿Qué pasa? ¿Qué pasa?"

"Shot him in the back."

"Happened in the stairwell."

"I seen it. He ran and the cop shot him in the back."

"You couldn't've seen. It was in the stairwell."

Marisol clutched Luis's hand. "Why're they burning the tire?"

"'Cause the cops wasted somebody."

"But—but the house could catch fire! What if . . . Why are they—?"

"No one's burning up houses; this ain't L.A." Luis shook her off impatiently. "It's a protest. We gotta show 'em! They can't come down here and— Who'd they get?"

More people running up. Eddie. Juan Ortiz. "¿Qué pasa?"

"A cop killed Castro."

Johnny Castro! The screaming woman was his grandmother! Mrs. Viega and another woman were holding her up.

Marisol, coatless, was shaking in the cold. Please, not Johnny. She saw him swinging a yo-yo; she saw his slow, easy smile. He was fifteen, like Luis. A kid, like her and Luis.

"Castro," Luis whispered. He looked both wounded and furious, the way he'd looked last summer when those cops roughed him up.

"They shot him in the stomach," someone was saying.

"No, in the heart. Hector seen him in the ambulance."

Acrid fumes filled Marisol's nose. Kids weren't supposed to die!

". . . 'cause he was *boricua*."

Because he was Puerto Rican? Marisol didn't want that to be true. No one could hate her that much for no reason at all. Could they?

". . . wouldn't shoot no Anglo, no matter how much he's carrying . . ."

Anger passed from person to person, building and building. Marisol felt it too; rage filled her chest.

The handful of cops shifted uneasily, eyes darting, hands on holsters, billy clubs poised.

"Go home," Luis said to her. "Before it breaks loose."

Marisol couldn't move. It was like a scary movie when she knew the worst part was coming; she'd want to look away, but her eyes had to stay on the screen.

Teenagers she didn't know, not from the block, came running up. "Pigs!" Their eyes glittered with excitement. "Get off our street!"

The cops swung into action. "Break it up! Get moving!" Someone got whacked with a club. Someone's forehead was bleeding. "Move it!"

"Hey man, I live here!"

People retreated and regrouped in a ragged ballet.

Blood streaming through someone's fingers. Bright red like make-believe Halloween blood. Like when Hector went as a vampire and put it on his teeth. . . .

"You!" Thump. "Get moving!"

"¡Hijo de——!"

"Party's over. Break it up!"

She was being shoved back and forth with the flow.

One of the cops looked like Sipowicz on NYPD Blue, Marisol thought. That was TV. This was real. Then why did everything *feel* so unreal?

"Killer cops!" The chant began. "Killer cops! Get off Loisada!"

Luis was with his friends now, his face distorted with fury in the streetlamp's light.

Marisol, shivering, moved to the edge of the crowd, close to familiar grown-ups.

"Killer cops!" Garbage can covers were banged in time to the chant. The rhythm was catchy enough to dance to, Marisol thought, but it would have to be all grotesque angles and stamping, full of bad feeling and danger. She was a million miles from Madame now.

"He had a knife," a woman near her said.

"No, they said a gun," Mr. Rodriguez said. "They said self-defense."

"They didn't need to kill him." Mr. Marin's voice was choked.

Someone threw a bottle. It crashed in the street, spewing soda into the air.

Johnny's grandmother was doubled over. Only the women around her kept her from sagging to the sidewalk. She was wrapped in a terry-cloth bathrobe. So she hadn't even been dressed when—

And then Papi was there. "You don't belong out here," he told Marisol. "Go home."

"Papi!" she wailed. She clutched his arm. "It was Johnny Castro!"

"I know, I heard." He held her for a moment. "Go inside, mi *tesoro*."

She shivered and couldn't move.

"Where's Luis?" Papi scanned the crowd and headed toward him. Over his shoulder, he repeated, "Inside, Marisol."

More police appeared. They moved forward slowly, in a straight line. With their riot gear, helmets, and plastic shields, they seemed to Marisol like aliens from a horror movie.

There was a frozen silence.

Marisol trailed after Papi, her eyes burning from the smoke. She was scared. She needed to be with Papi, but people were blocking the way.

Marisol heard his voice: "Luis! Get inside! Go home!" and Luis's defiant "No!"

"I said go home!"

"No! They killed Johnny Castro!" Luis raged.

"Listen to me! Use your brain." Papi grabbed Luis's arm. "We don't know what happened."

"They murdered him!" Luis shook off Papi's hand.

"This is your father talking: Get in the house. *Inmediatamente.*"

"No!"

Luis was disobeying in front of all the people on the street! Papi was mad as anything.

"Blockhead!" Papi took a breath. "There's twenty different rumors going around. Wait to find out and—"

Everybody could hear Papi and Luis arguing.

"That's right," Mr. Rodriguez called. "We gotta wait and find out—"

"Johnny didn't do nothing! They shot him down like a dog!" Luis's voice was harsh with emotion.

"Like a dog!" someone echoed. "Open season on Ricans."

"¡Tonto! You don't know what he'd do to save his stash. Too crazy-scared to lose it." Papi pointed into the darkness. "Too scared of his boss over there."

Marisol followed his gesture toward Tito. He was with his crew, in the shadows, slouched against a brick wall, coolly observing the scene. The dog was on a tight leash at his side.

A chill crawled along Marisol's neck. She felt small and helpless. She worked her way close to Papi and Luis.

"Antonio's right," a man yelled. "Listen to him."

"Killer cops! Get them off Loisada!" a voice shouted. "Come on!"

"Don't be stupid!" Papi yelled at the crowd. "You want a riot? You wanta burn your own block?"

"Not for a dealer," a man's voice growled.

The grandmother's voice cut through, high-pitched and shaking. "He was a good boy, my Juanito. He was a good boy."

"I'm sorry, *señora*." Papi's hand went over his heart. "*Lo siento*." He looked sadder than Marisol had ever seen him.

"¡Justicia! ¡Justicia!"

The police moved forward slowly, in line, poised and ready.

On both sides of the street, people were hanging out of their windows and out on the fire escapes. The police kept looking up, scanning the rooftops.

A rock was hurled and the streetlight shattered. For a moment, only the dying flames on the tire lit the street. Faces became shadowed, reflecting orange and blue.

Avenue C was no longer the street Marisol knew. In the darkness neighbors looked like strangers. Bodies were rushing here and there, directionless, in jumpy silhouette. Someone ran by and bumped against her; rough wool scraped against her arm. Her mouth tasted of burned rubber.

Suddenly everything became bright white in the glare of police spotlights.

No one moved. There was a last moment, a last intake of breath, before the explosion that was waiting to break loose.

"¡Justicia! ¡Venganza!" Marisol saw Eddie in the crowd, his lips drawn back in a snarl.

"Not like this!" Papi was in the middle of the street now. "We got kids to raise here. We don't need to lose another one!"

"Listen to him," Mr. Rodriguez called. "Stay calm."

Someone screamed a curse and spit on the ground.

"Get going!" A policeman shoved Juan Ortiz. "Break it up!"

Kids were running everywhere and doubling back.

"¡Oye!" Nina Matos's hair shone neon yellow in the white light. "Hear what Antonio says!"

"¡Justicia! ¡Venganza!" People raised their fists and shook them in the air.

"You want *venganza*? I'll show you who killed Johnny Castro!" Papi shouted. "¡Mira! Over there."

In the shadows, Tito uncoiled from his casual slouch. He stood erect and alert, like an animal sniffing the air. His crew straightened up around him. The dog strained forward.

Papi couldn't talk against Tito, not out loud! Tito had the power! In blind panic, Marisol edged to Luis's side; her brother was tight with tension.

"You know who's killing our kids," Papi continued hoarsely. "Killing our neighborhood. Get him off Loisada!"

"Tell it, Antonio!"

"No, Papi, please," Marisol tried to say, but her voice wouldn't work. Even Luis, right next to her, couldn't hear her.

Tito's voice cut through, calm and cold. "You're asking to get popped, little man."

Marisol saw Mrs. Ortega cross herself and mouth, "¡Ay, Dios mío!" Mrs. Ortega, too, knew that something terrible was about to happen! Marisol's whole body clutched.

"We gotta get together, all of us, and *do* it," Papi shouted. "Take back our streets!"

Luis's face was white and drawn. "He's got to stop. We gotta shut him up."

He darted through the crowd and grabbed at Papi's arm. Then Mr. Marin was there, his arm around Papi's shoulders.

"Loisada don't have to be a dope market!" Papi shouted. "No more Johnny Castros!"

Papi was too hotheaded; he was going to say more! Marisol was paralyzed with fear. She couldn't breathe.

Time stopped. Close-up details jumped out at her. She saw every turquoise on Tito's silver belt buckle. She saw the drop of saliva threading its way from the dog's mouth.

She whispered a fragmented prayer through numb lips.

Tito took a step forward and the light caught his face. It was a mask that showed nothing. His eyes were focused on Papi. They were like jagged tin.

Luis and Mr. Marin were pulling Papi away from the center. She saw Luis talking and talking at him, tugging at him. Finally, he really *looked* at Luis and his shoulders slumped as he nodded. The humiliation of backing down was all over his face.

Marisol watched Tito stare at them for an endless moment. Then he laughed contemptuously. When his posture relaxed, Marisol's knees gave way with relief.

She felt light-headed. She pushed past the people surrounding Papi. She reached for his hand and held on tight. Papi looked down at her with a tired smile and touched her hair.

"All right, break it up." The cops were moving knots of people around. "Go home."

Nina Matos was standing on a parked car. "Go home and get candles!" she called. "A protest march to the precinct!"

The crowd shifted and murmured.

"A peaceful march," Mr. Rodriguez yelled to the police. "There's no riot here tonight."

Late that night, Marisol carried a candle next to Luis. She kept her hand cupped over it, to protect it from the wind. Many candles flickered ahead of her and behind her. There was a long line of people, slowly walking through the hushed streets to the police station. Papi and Nina Matos were near the front with some other men.

The mood of rage had given way to sorrow.

"I keep remembering Johnny from long ago," Marisol whispered. "He was always nice to me."

"He had a good heart," Luis said.

"Why did that have to happen to him?"

"We're gonna get some answers. I ain't leaving till we get answers," Luis said.

"The things Papi said. That was the truth."

"I know."

Shuffling feet filled the night.

"You think writing down license numbers is gonna mean anything?" Marisol asked. Papi and the others were organizing to take turns on the street, to scare off the uptown cars that lined up to buy from Tito's crew. Some even had Jersey plates.

"I don't know." Luis's voice sounded thick. He had trouble clearing his throat.

"You're scared for Papi," she said.

Luis nodded.

"You couldn't work for someone who'd hurt a man like Papi. You wouldn't—"

"No," Luis said. "No, I can't."

The solemn procession turned the corner. Marisol heard someone sobbing softly.

"Another R.I.P. mural for Chico to paint," Luis said sadly.

Marisol's eyes were wet. "It could have been you."

● ● ●

Jeanne Carlsen called the next evening. "Are you all right, Marisol? I saw on the news. What's going on down there?"

"Nothing. It's quiet." An investigation had been promised and the people were waiting to see. And there was talk against Johnny Castro—he was selling, he'd asked for it, he was no innocent angel. . . . Maybe that was all true, but it made Marisol feel terrible.

"Are we on for Sunday? I'll pick you up at—"

"No, don't pick me up," Marisol said quickly. "I'll meet you someplace; don't come here."

There was a pause. "It's okay. I wouldn't be in uniform."

"But people know you're a—"

"All right. I'll meet you."

"I still like you," Marisol blurted. "I'm not blaming you. But they didn't have to go and kill him! I knew him, I knew he was messed up, but . . . He lived upstairs with his grandma and . . . He wasn't a monster."

"I don't know exactly how it happened," Jeanne said slowly. "I hear that Castro drew a weapon. That makes it self-defense, Marisol."

"People are saying it's 'cause he was Puerto Rican. The cop could have shot him in the arm or— Why did he have to—"

"Maybe he overreacted from fear. Maybe it was by the book. I don't know what went down in that stairwell. I can't say I wouldn't have done the same thing."

"But Johnny was only—"

"Makes no difference if the hand holding the gun is fifteen or fifty. There's a split second that decides if you're going home to your family that night."

"But he was only a kid."

"We're not the enemy, Marisol. There *are* bad cops out there, but honestly, most of us do a hard job the very best way we can."

"I know," Marisol said, "but it hurts."

She wished there was something beautiful for her to escape to. But that was over. She didn't have the heart to even look in the ballet book anymore.

By the next week, the neighborhood had returned to normal. Luis worked at Isla Verde every day after school. Papi covered his restaurant shifts. Mikey Santiago, a bright-eyed fourteen-year-old, replaced Johnny Castro in Tito's network.

By Wednesday, Desirée's absence in Mrs. Lonigan's class hardly made a dent—she had been so quiet, no one but Marisol missed her at all. Iris Muñoz moved up a row into Desirée's old seat.

The first ballet class after vacation would go on as usual that afternoon, Marisol thought. Pliés, port de bras, relevés, ronds de jambe, the regular routine, uninterrupted, with or without the presence of Marisol Perez. Maybe Desirée and Claire would wonder about her for a while. Maybe Madame would notice her absence for about a minute. But then everyone would spread out at the barre and there'd be no space where she used to stand. Picturing it broke her heart.

After school, Marisol followed Gloria out of the classroom with leaden resignation.

Ballet wasn't life or death, she thought. She could have lost Papi in the blink of an eye if it had gone the wrong way that nightmarish night. But she still had him. And Luis too. So she wouldn't cry for what she couldn't have. Maybe that's what growing up was about. Papi wasn't crying about not working as a guitarist. Not on the outside, anyway.

"It's too bad about your dancing." Gloria looked sympathetic.

Marisol took her time on the stairs. She felt dull and empty. She didn't have to rush to be anyplace at four.

"Anyway, you learned all those exercises," Gloria said, "so you can do them on your own. And," she continued cheerfully, "you won't even have to take the subway."

"It's not like that," Marisol said. "I need Madame's corrections and . . . If you keep working the wrong way, it could ruin your muscles forever and . . ." Oh, what was the use of explaining?

"It's so funny, the way you call that lady 'Madame.'"

They entered the room for the after-school program.

"If you wanna go to the art table, I'll go with you," Gloria volunteered.

"All right." Anything but knitting.

Marisol unzipped her jacket and mechanically tossed it on a corner of the table. Madame was going to start them on pirouettes; she wondered if it would be this afternoon.

The chairs scraped as the girls sat down. Marisol settled into hers.

Anyway, she could still get *Swan Lake* from the library. Not yet. Sometime later, when it wouldn't hurt so much.

Marisol got up to get some clay. She rolled it into a ball in her hands. She tried to think of something to make. She tried really hard to get interested. . . .

"Yo! Marisol!" Luis was in the doorway.

She looked up, surprised.

"Move it if you wanta get there at four!"

"What? But—"

"You got to go home and get your stuff!"

"My leotard?" she whispered. "My slippers?"

"Come on, I'm taking you."

"You are? Luis? You mean it?"

"Hurry up, you're gonna be late."

She grabbed her jacket. She flew out of the room and down the front stairs.

They ran toward home. "What happened? What about your job?" she asked breathlessly.

"You know Frankie, my friend with the limp? I got him to take Wednesdays for me. Mr. Rivera said okay."

"Oh! Oh! Oh, Luis!"

They raced up the street. Marisol was sure her feet weren't touching the ground at all!

At home, Marisol threw her things into a bag. They ran all the way to the subway and jumped on the train just as the doors were about to close.

"Whew," Marisol said.

Even Luis was breathing hard.

He checked his new Swatch. "You'll make it. Maybe a couple of minutes late."

"No problem," she gasped. She could brave Madame's raised eyebrows if she straggled in late. She could handle anything now!

They flopped down on seats. By the next stop they had stopped panting.

"Thank you, you saved my life!" she said.

He smiled. "*De nada.*"

"You're gonna take me every Wednesday?"

He nodded. "But I don't wanta set no more speed records down East Houston."

"Mr. Rivera's gonna cut your pay," she said.

"Yeah, well."

"I'm sorry. Thanks a million! I'm sorry I . . ."

It was a big responsibility, she thought, to have someone sacrifice for you.

"Luis . . . I don't know if I'm that good. I don't know for sure if I can be a dancer. I think I can, but—"

"It's all right," he said. "It's good you have a dream."

More people got on at Twenty-third Street. An obese man sat down next to Marisol—he took up a seat and a half, and she squeezed closer to Luis.

"There's another problem," Marisol said. "Next year, class is twice a week. And then advanced level is even more. . . ." That was the red leotards. She had to wear a red leotard one day!

"Look, by then you could go by yourself."

"You think Papi—?"

"You'll be a year older, won't you? Papi'll come

around."

"You think so?"

"You take after him; you're doing things he wishes he could've, not *ballet*, but . . . you make him happy. He tried to get his day off switched to Wednesdays, you know that? It didn't work with the schedule, but he tried."

"He never told me." Papi would have given his day off to her! And Luis—if he saved her life in a fire, that would be one-time heroics; giving her all those Wednesday afternoons stretching ahead of them, that was really something!

She wanted to tell him how much she loved him back. So she punched his arm and said, "Hey, bro."

"So I'll show you the way," Luis continued, "and you'll learn it backwards and forwards, and—"

"I know it backwards and forwards now."

"—and I'll talk to him. It'll be okay, you'll be old enough."

"Luis—you ought to have a dream too."

"I know, I'm looking for one." His voice became so soft that she could hardly hear over the rattle of the subway.

Thirty-fourth Street. The doors slid open and closed. The train rumbled out of the station and picked up speed.

He got up. "Forty-second Street's next. Here's where you change."

"Duh. I know." As if she hadn't been leading the Joliecoeurs all this time!

She followed him off the train.

"Pay attention," he said. "You go up these stairs here."

"Right."

They waited on the other platform.

"If it's late when you come home and there's no other people around, you wait by the token booth, okay? 'Cause if there's trouble, they got a direct line to the police."

"The trains are jammed when I come home. It's rush hour!"

"But in case you ever get hung up and it gets late. Just so you know. You listening?"

"Okay, okay."

They took the Seven to Times Square.

"If any guy around here talks to you, freeze him," Luis said. "Walk away."

"I know what to do." She smiled. "Anyway, nobody's gonna bother with me."

"You're getting too pretty, you got to be careful."

Her smile became wider and wider.

Luis checked his watch. "Twenty of four."

She dug in her bag, took out the sweatband, and pulled it over her hair. If only she could change on the subway!

They ran off the train and toward the Broadway line.

"Come on, we can make it." Luis tugged at her as the express came roaring and screeching into the station.

She pulled back. "No, we've got to wait for the local. Lincoln Center's a local stop."

"Oh." He got busy slicking back his hair. "And another thing, don't lean over the platform looking for the train."

"I'm only like half a mile from the edge."

Finally they came out of the subway and into the bustle of Broadway.

Luis looked around quickly, trying to hide his confusion.

"See over there"—Marisol pointed—"that's the Metropolitan Opera. My school's right behind it, off Amsterdam."

Marisol led the way. There it all was: the Juilliard School, Avery Fisher Hall, the banners, the theaters, the restaurants, a glimpse of crystal chandeliers through the glass doors of the Met, the broad plaza, and her beautiful, beautiful fountain, even if it *was* turned off. She had come home again!

She was so filled with joy that she couldn't stand it. She took a running start and made three perfect jetés across the plaza.